*Whose perfect guy?*

"I know we only met Herbert tonight, but I'm telling you—he's the one for me," I sighed. "It's like fate, you know? I suggested we come up here this weekend, and here's this guy who's perfect for me in every way—"

"Perfect for *you*?" Jessica exclaimed, looking baffled.

"Well, yeah," I said defensively.

"What makes you so sure? You don't even know him," Jessica said.

I sighed impatiently. She's never been logical in her entire life. Why was she starting now? "I can just tell, that's all," I said. "It's like a sixth sense. Jessica, you had to notice the way he kept staring at me when he was singing tonight. I mean, he was looking at me almost the whole time."

Jessica frowned. "I wouldn't say he was looking at you the *whole* time. Actually, I'm pretty sure he caught my eye—"

Bantam Books in THE UNICORN CLUB series.
Ask your bookseller for the books you have missed.

Coming soon:

# THE UNICORN CLUB

# KIMBERLY RIDES AGAIN

Written by
Alice Nicole Johansson

Created by
FRANCINE PASCAL

BANTAM BOOKS
NEW YORK • TORONTO • LONDON • SYDNEY • AUCKLAND

RL 4, 008-012

KIMBERLY RIDES AGAIN
A Bantam Book / November 1995

Sweet Valley High® and The Unicorn Club®
are registered trademarks of Francine Pascal

Conceived by Francine Pascal

Produced by Daniel Weiss Associates, Inc.
33 West 17th Street
New York, NY 10011

Cover art by James Mathewuse

ISBN: 0-553-48352-8
Published simultaneously in the United States and Canada

Bantam Books are published by Bantam Books, a division of Bantam
Doubleday Dell Publishing Group, Inc. Its trademark, consisting of the
words "Bantam Books" and the portrayal of a rooster, is Registered in U.S.
Patent and Trademark Office and in other countries. Marca Registrada.
Bantam Books, 1540 Broadway, New York, New York 10036.

PRINTED IN THE UNITED STATES OF AMERICA

OPM     0 9 8 7 6 5 4 3 2 1

112734

*To Ada Szeto and Michael Rubin*

# One

My name is Kimberly Haver, and it was all my idea, from the very beginning. Let me just say that right up front.

I saw a magazine article all about this dude ranch, and I mentioned it to my parents, pointing out that a weekend at the dude ranch with my friends just might be the best way for me to get back into the swing of things in Sweet Valley. See, I'd only been back from Atlanta for a couple of weeks. In case you didn't know, my family had moved to Atlanta for a little while, because my dad's job got transferred there.

Talk about bad luck. I guess there were *some* cool people in Atlanta, but I really missed the Unicorn Club. And while I was gone, the club took a major nosedive, hanging out with a bunch of boring girls who now call themselves the Angels.

Which brings me back to my first point. I figured that spending a weekend at this dude ranch seemed like the perfect way to get me and the Unicorn Club back on the right track. It turned out my parents had actually been to this dude ranch a couple of times on vacations, and so they liked the idea.

And me? I love horses, and I've been riding since I was six. The fact that my dad was springing for the whole trip had everyone in a great mood that Wednesday afternoon, when we got together at my house to finalize our plans.

"Kimberly, do you have any ranch dressing or anything to go with these?" Jessica Wakefield asked me, as she held up a large bag of rippled potato chips. Jessica has long blond hair and pretty blue-green eyes.

"Jessica, how can you even think about eating ranch dressing?" Lila Fowler made a disgusted face and tossed her long brown hair over her shoulder.

"On potato chips?" Jessica said.

"On *anything*." Lila looked as though she was about to get sick. "Euw."

"Come on, it's great," Jessica declared. "Try some on the carrot sticks, if you don't want chips."

I handed her the bottle of dressing from the refrigerator, and Jessica dumped a huge dollop out onto the plate beside the carrots I'd cut up. She held the plate out to Lila. "You'd better get used to ranch dressing—I mean, what else are they going to have on a dude ranch?"

"I prefer raspberry vinaigrette, if you don't mind," Lila said, picking up a carrot and crunching it lightly between her teeth.

"Well, la-dee-da," Jessica replied, frowning at her as she dunked a small potato chip into the ranch dressing and popped it into her mouth.

I grinned. I was used to hearing Jessica and Lila argue like this. They've been best friends for as long as I can remember, but sometimes their friendship is kind of, well, maybe *explosive* is a good word for it. Lila's family is incredibly wealthy. She lives in a mansion with servants, a pool, and just about everything you could ask for. She has a million clothes and a brand-new stereo system, and she gets a facial practically every other week.

Jessica's an identical twin, but she's almost nothing like her sister, Elizabeth. Elizabeth was a Unicorn for a little while, but if you ask me, she's all wrong for the club—way too boring and goody-goody. In fact, now she belongs to the Angels. Figures.

Besides me, Jessica, and Lila, the only other official member of the Unicorn Club is Ellen Riteman. Ellen's got short, light brown hair and blue eyes, and the major thing you have to know about her is that she's a little on the spacey side. Like, if you don't remind her to take a left when you're riding your bikes home from the mall, she misses her house completely. But she's incredibly nice, and probably the most faithful friend in the world.

I like faithfulness, especially when it comes to

the Unicorns. See, we've had our problems sticking together. My mom says that's only natural, but I don't like it. I don't understand why everyone can't just get along, and if sometimes that means putting up with stuff you don't like, then tough. That's life. I mean, did I *want* to move to Atlanta and leave all my friends behind? No. I just had to do it.

Just like I had to make sure that everyone in the Unicorn Club knew who was in charge now. Me.

(What can I say? I'm a Leo. I was practically born to be in charge.)

"So we're still planning to leave for the dude ranch on Friday, as soon as school's out," I announced to Jessica, Lila, and Ellen, who were all perched on stools around the counter island in my kitchen. "My father's borrowing one of his company's vans, and he'll pick us up there."

"Ugh. Do I actually have to bring my suitcase to school?" Lila asked, setting her glass of juice on the counter. "I hate that."

"I know," Ellen added. "Besides, I'm not sure if I can carry mine on my bike."

I looked at Jessica and rolled my eyes. "Really, you guys. He's going to get your stuff *first*. Then he'll come to get us. OK?"

Ellen laughed. "Right."

"What's the name of the place we're going to again?" Jessica asked. "I need to brag about it to my brother a few more times."

"The Sunset Dude Ranch," I told her. "It's a couple hours north of here, in the mountains. And it's a very in place to go."

"I've already bought a whole new wardrobe, so there'd better be some dudes—and cute ones," Lila added.

"What did you get?" Ellen asked.

"Well, there's the purple cowboy hat I picked up at Western Outfitters at the mall . . . a new denim shirt with one of those metal tie things . . ."

"A bolo, you mean?" I asked her.

Lila nodded. "But the best thing of all is my new pair of gray alligator-skin boots."

"Cool," Ellen said.

"Alligator? You're actually going to wear a reptile?" Jessica asked. "That's cruel."

I shot Jessica a glance. "Since when did you become so concerned about animals?" I pointed at her leather sandals. "Correct me if I'm wrong, but I don't think those sandals are made out of canvas or anything."

Lila laughed, and Jessica stuck out her tongue at her. "I still say wearing alligator boots is weird."

"Maybe it's a little weird, but it's fashionable," Lila insisted. "And if there are any cute boys hanging around, I want to make sure they notice me."

"Don't worry," I said. "I bet there will be lots of boys." I sighed, thinking about the great weekend ahead of us. "But boys aren't the *only* reason we're going," I reminded my friends. "I personally can't wait to go riding, out in the wilderness. And it'll be great to hang out together, especially since *this* time we won't have the measles."

"No kidding," Ellen agreed. "I thought we were all going to go crazy!"

The four of us had been quarantined at Lila's house a few weeks back when we'd all come down with the measles. I felt as if I was just finally getting over the entire, awful experience—first, being cooped up at someone else's house for days on end, and second, having a bunch of incredibly irritating red spots all over me.

"Well, all I know is, I'm glad I wasn't stuck at your house during that measles thing with the Angels," I told Jessica.

"Yeah, no kidding," Lila replied. "I mean, Jessica's house doesn't have fourteen bedrooms, does it?"

"Well, ex*cuse* me for not being a millionaire," Jessica retorted.

"It's not that," I said. "It's being quarantined with *them*."

The Angels, that is. You see, they just so happened to have the measles at the same time we did (I guess that's one of the very, very few things we have in common), and *they* were quarantined at the Wakefields'.

"Yeah, I guess that wouldn't have been too much fun," Ellen said. "They're so boring."

"Elizabeth isn't boring," Jessica protested. "And neither is Mandy." She stared out the kitchen window and sighed. "I miss Mandy sometimes, you know?"

"Yeah," Ellen added, nodding. "Me too."

"You know, it's really too bad about Mandy becoming an Angel," I mused. "I don't know how she can stand hanging out with those goody-goodies. I mean, I always thought she was a lot more fun than that, and way cooler. But if she wants to spend her time sitting around thinking up different ways to help old ladies cross the street, I guess we can't stop her."

I liked Mandy, but if she was going to choose the wrong club to be in, I didn't know how much longer I was supposed to consider myself 'her friend. She sure hadn't acted like a friend when she chose the Angels over the Unicorns.

Lila cleared her throat. "Actually? I was thinking about Mandy, and there's something I want to suggest."

"I want to talk about Mandy, too," Jessica said, sitting up in her chair. "It's about her and the Unicorn Club."

"What's to discuss?" I said, shrugging. "How she blew her chance to be a Unicorn? I mean, we can talk about it, but it's not going to *do* anything, or change the fact that—"

"I want to give her another chance," Jessica said, interrupting me.

"I want to invite Mandy to come with us this weekend," Lila said, at exactly the same time.

I felt as if I was going to fall off my chair. "*What* did you guys just say?" I demanded.

"They want to invite Mandy to come with us this weekend," Ellen patiently repeated.

"I heard what they said," I told Ellen, exasperated. "I just don't believe them!" I set my glass down on the table so hard that I almost broke it.

"Well . . ." Lila said uncertainly, "I've been thinking about Mandy a lot lately. And I guess . . . I don't know. I miss her."

Jessica nodded. "I talked to her for a second in class today, and I think she misses us, too."

"So?" I tossed my long brown hair over my shoulder. "Of course she does. She's hanging out with a boring crowd." Maybe I sound a little harsh when it comes to the Angels, but believe me, I have my reasons. Did I mention that Mary Wallace won the student council election over me because of Mandy? And that they act like they're better than everyone else, just because they do a lot of volunteer work? *I* should have been student council president. OK, so I probably shouldn't have stolen Mary's speech and used it as my own, but that didn't mean I should have lost. Life is so unfair sometimes!

"Maybe Mandy's sick of being an Angel," Ellen suggested. "She might not be having as much fun as she seems to be."

"Yeah, and if she misses us as much as we miss her, then maybe she would want to come along on our dude ranch weekend," Jessica said.

"I'll even pay for her share," Lila offered, "if your dad can't."

I stared at her, not knowing what to say. Money wasn't the problem—I knew we'd be sharing a suite, and having one more person along wouldn't make a big difference there. But did they expect me to accept Mandy back into my life, just like that? I mean, I'll admit I really considered her a friend at one point, and there *are* some cool things about her, but I couldn't just forget about the fact that she chose the Angels over us. Not right now, anyway.

"What do you think, Kimberly?" Jessica asked. "You're the one who should decide."

"I bet we'd have a great time up in the mountains together," Ellen pressed. "You know Mandy—she's always up for any kind of adventure. And she gives great fashion advice!"

"Plus, she'd be totally grateful to you for inviting her along," Lila added. "Because it's an incredibly generous offer, in case we haven't already thanked you a hundred times."

"Yeah." Jessica beamed at me. "You're doing this really nice thing for all of us—I'm sure Mandy would totally appreciate it."

"Hm. I don't know." I thought about it for a second. They *were* making some pretty good points. Mandy would be fun on a trip—she was always cracking jokes, and she'd do almost anything on a dare. Hanging out with us would be good for her—maybe it would remind her of which club she was really supposed to be in. And if she ended up being grateful to me . . . well, that might come in handy someday, if I needed her help with something. She *did* know a lot of boys at school.

"Think of it this way, Kimberly," Lila said, sounding excited. "If Mandy spends the weekend with us, maybe she'll decide she wants to be a Unicorn again! And you know what *that* means. We'd have *five* members, and the Angels would only have *four*." She looked at me and raised her eyebrows.

I felt my mouth form a small smile. I have to say, not only is Lila extremely rich—she's extremely smart, too. Winning Mandy away from the Angels would be a *major* coup. The more I thought of it, the more I liked the idea. Having Mandy back in the Unicorns would be good for our image—she's a very funky dresser, she's funny, and those two things make her incredibly popular at school. And on top of that, I knew it would just kill the Angels if Mandy decided she'd rather be a Unicorn instead. "Well, when you guys put it that way, it sounds like a pretty good idea to ask Mandy to come with us," I finally said.

"All right!" Jessica and Lila slapped each other a high five. Ellen tried to join them, but they lowered their hands and she ended up smacking her palm against the wall instead.

"Um . . . way to go, wall!" Ellen said with a shrug, and we all laughed.

I couldn't wait for our dude ranch weekend. I especially couldn't wait to try to convince Mandy that we were the only club at Sweet Valley Middle School worth belonging to.

It was kind of like the way my dad describes his business deals: a win-win situation.

# Two

After school let out the next day, Jessica and I caught up with Mandy out in front, while she was unlocking her bicycle from the rack in the parking lot. "Hey, Mandy!" Jessica said cheerfully as we walked up to her. "Can we talk to you about something?"

"I can't talk long," Mandy said, pulling her old green three-speed out of the rack. That's Mandy for you—even her bike is funky, with streamers coming out of the handlebars, an old-fashioned metal bell, and a wicker basket. It looks like the bike the witch rode in *The Wizard of Oz*. "I have to get to the day-care center."

"Oh, this won't take long," I promised her. "We have a little proposition for you."

"Not a little one—an incredibly fun one," Jessica said, correcting me. "Mandy, how would you like to spend this weekend in the most glorious, exciting, fantastic place, with four of your best friends?"

"What is this, a game show? No, wait—we tried that already." Mandy grimaced. She was talking about the *Best Friends* TV game show, which the Unicorns had been on during the time I lived in Atlanta.

"No, silly, it's not a game show," Jessica said, punching Mandy lightly on the arm. "It's a weekend at the Sunset Dude Ranch, up in the mountains, and Kimberly's parents are paying for the whole, entire thing!"

Mandy's eyes widened. "Wow. Sunsets and dudes included?"

I laughed. "I hope so. Anyway, we want you to come with us."

"Really?" Mandy said. She sounded amazed. "But what about me being, you know . . ."

"An Angel?" I spat out. Saying that word always gave me the creeps. I mean, who did they think they were, calling themselves angels?

"Yeah," Mandy said. "I didn't think that Unicorns and Angels were supposed to, you know, socialize."

"Well, technically, probably not," I answered. I definitely didn't want to socialize with the whole group, that was for sure! "But we decided to make an exception just this once, just for you, because we want you to come."

"We all really want you to come along," Jessica added in her best pleading voice.

"We're leaving tomorrow, after school," I went

on. "My dad's going to drive—all you need to do is ask your parents' permission, get them to sign a consent form, and then we're off for a whole weekend of riding. OK? Can you be ready by two thirty?"

"Well . . . I don't know," Mandy said, fiddling with the streamers on her handlebars.

"You don't know?" Jessica sounded appalled. "How can you not know? We're talking about the same dude ranch that was featured in *Teen Talk* in that article on 'Way-Cool California Vacations' last month. It doesn't *get* any better than that."

"Oh, it's that ranch?" Mandy asked. "The one up in the mountains, with the rustic stuff?"

I nodded. "Yeah, that's it. And we have an entire suite to ourselves. No parents, no homework—"

"And tons of boys," Jessica added. "With any luck, that is. Come on, Mandy, you can't say no. Unless, of course, you don't like horseback riding, which I can't believe, since it's only the coolest thing to *do* at a dude ranch."

Mandy bit her lip. "Riding, huh? Like, all day?"

I nodded eagerly. "Yeah, it's going to be incredible. You *do* ride, don't you?"

"Oh, sure," Mandy said quickly. "Actually, I love horseback riding. First off, you get to wear all of the hippest clothes, and second, there's the thrill of the open trail—"

"I think you mean the open road," I said.

Mandy waved her hand in the air. "Whatever. All I know is, I'm practically Dale Evans when it comes to horses. Hi-ho, Silver and all that."

"Really? I didn't know that," Jessica said. "You never mentioned it before."

"Sure I did," Mandy said. "Haven't you seen the huge collection of horse books in my room?"

"No. But never mind—it's settled," Jessica declared. "You're coming!"

"Well . . . maybe," Mandy said. "I might have to check and see if the Angels have anything scheduled for this weekend. Something they might need me for."

"I doubt it," Jessica said. "I was talking to Elizabeth earlier, and she said she and Maria are spending the weekend at a school newspaper workshop, if you can imagine anything as boring as *that*. And I think she mentioned something about Mary going away to her grandmother's house in San Francisco."

"Oh, that's right—I almost forgot," Mandy said. "And Evie has a violin concert in Los Angeles that she's performing in, so I guess that leaves me without much of a weekend at all."

"But that's where you're wrong," I said, "because you're spending the weekend with us!"

"We're going to have so much fun," Jessica said excitedly. "We've already decided that this is going to be one of the best weekends in Unicorn history."

Mandy looked a little uneasy. "Yeah. I guess so. Only I'm not a Unicorn," she said.

"True," I agreed. "But look at it this way. Just because we're not in the same club, that doesn't mean we can't be friends anymore. *Some* of us, anyway."

Mandy frowned at me. "Some of us?"

"You know—the ones who get along the best, like you and me," I said. "It would be silly to pretend not to be friends after all *we've* been through together."

"Kimberly's right," Jessica said. "I mean, that'd be like me and Elizabeth not talking, just because she's an Angel and I'm a Unicorn. Of course we can still be friends, silly."

"But you guys are sisters," Mandy said. "Twin, identical, share the same parents, live in the same house, have the same skin type, sisters. That's different. Are you sure you guys want me to come?"

"Of course we're sure," I said. "Don't be ridiculous. We talked about it yesterday at our meeting, and the vote was unanimous. Really, Mandy. I'm starting to think you don't *want* to come."

"No—I do!" Mandy said. "But can you call me tonight with all the details? Right now I have to take off for the Center. Unless you guys want to come along—then we could talk about it on the way or something." She got onto her bike.

"I don't think so," I said, smoothing my hair behind my ear. I wasn't trying to be snobby, but my idea of fun doesn't include spending the afternoon baby-sitting a bunch of kids. Especially not if the Angels are going to be there. They think they even know how to baby-sit better than me, which is totally ridiculous. I could be a great baby-sitter, if I wanted to be. It's just that I have better things to do with my time. It's called a social life.

"What about you, Jessica? Want to come? I know Oliver would love to see you," Mandy urged. At least she didn't bug me to come along—I had to give her credit for that.

Jessica sighed. "I haven't seen him in a whole week. I feel awful."

"Then come with me," Mandy suggested. "It's the perfect no-guilt plan. Besides, it'll be fun."

"I do really miss him," Jessica said thoughtfully. Then she grinned. "OK, I'll come! Sure you don't want to come, Kimberly?"

"Oh, I'm sure," I muttered to Jessica. "The less time I spend with *them*, the better."

Mandy frowned. "*Them*, meaning the Angels? If that's how you feel about them, then I'm not sure I should come—"

"No, no!" I quickly interrupted her. "I didn't mean it the way it sounded. I just—you know, have a lot to do this afternoon, and so I can't come because I don't have the *time*. But you guys have fun, and I'll see you tomorrow, OK?" I turned around and started walking home before Mandy could say anything more.

As I neared home, I was almost skipping, I was in such a great mood. Mandy had agreed to come, and that meant we were halfway toward getting her back into the Unicorns. I could see the five of us now— me, Lila, Jessica, Ellen, and Mandy—parading into school on Monday morning, arms wrapped around one another's shoulders.

Just thinking about how the Angels would react to that made me smile.

"You guys are not going to believe this," Lila said, sliding into a chair across the table from me at lunch on Friday.

"Don't tell me," I teased her, peeling the top off a container of banana-strawberry yogurt. "You couldn't decide what to pack for this weekend, so you're having your whole closet shipped up to the dude ranch?"

"*No*," Lila said, frowning at me. "I did have trouble narrowing things down to three bags, but what I have to tell you is much more exciting. Much more." She calmly sipped from her bottle of apple juice. "It's about Janet."

Janet Howell is Lila's cousin. She's in the ninth grade at Sweet Valley High, and she's the one who actually founded the Unicorn Club. It was thanks to Janet that we had our own special spot in the lunchroom, called, naturally, the Unicorner. She'd made it obvious to everyone that this was our table, and no one else ever tried to sit at it. Janet had a way of telling people what to do that I've always admired. Like, you just accepted what she said, and then you realized she was basically bossing you around. But it was OK, because she was usually *right*.

"So what's up with Janet?" I asked Lila. "Wait,

don't tell me—she got to be student council president her first year, right?"

"No, not exactly." Lila lowered her voice dramatically. "It's bad news. Heartbreaking, actually."

"Oh, no," Ellen said. "What happened? She's OK, isn't she?"

"She might be—someday," Lila said.

"What is it already?" Jessica demanded.

"Yeah, the suspense is killing me," I said. Lila has a habit of drawing out these little stories into major murder mysteries. She'll tell you her arm is broken, and then it turns out she broke a *nail*.

"Well. Here's what happened." Lila set down her juice. "There's this guy she liked, a sophomore. His name's Chris Blake. He's supposed to be really cute, but I've never seen him or anything. Anyway, Janet had a huge crush on him."

"And he didn't like her back?" Ellen asked. "Ouch. I hate when that happens."

Lila shook her head. "No, it's worse than that. I've told you about her new best friend, Cindy, right?"

I nodded.

"Well, it turns out that Janet only knew about this Chris guy in the first place because Cindy liked him. And then Janet decided to go after Chris, too, and she started hanging out with him, and flirting, and pretty soon after that he asked Janet out—"

"And Cindy was furious," I guessed. I knew how I'd feel if Janet did that to me! If I were

Cindy, I probably wouldn't even talk to Janet again, much less forgive her. It was funny, because I'd almost never seen Janet do anything I didn't like. But this was way up there on the "Being a Lousy Friend" scale.

"Definitely furious," Lila agreed. "She's not even talking to Janet anymore, and on top of that, Chris told Janet he'd rather just be *friends*. Isn't that the most humiliating thing you've ever heard?"

"That sounds awful," Ellen agreed.

"Janet wouldn't stop crying when she was talking to me. It was really sad," Lila went on. "She's lost her best friend over some dumb guy. She told me I ought to be glad I had you guys as friends. Because we'd never go behind one another's backs or let some boy come between us like that."

"Are you kidding?" Ellen said. "Never. Not in a million years."

"I can't say that I actually sympathize with Janet. I mean, what she did was pretty stupid," I said. "I don't care how cute he is, it's not worth losing a friend over some guy."

"Hmm." Jessica was fidgeting with her straw, looking thoughtfully into space.

I raised an eyebrow at her. "What are you thinking, Jessica?"

"Well," she began, "what about if someone really great like . . . let's just imagine that Johnny Buck asked me out—when Ellen's the one who's been nuts about him for five years?"

"We'd have to imagine pretty hard," Lila commented with a smirk.

Jessica stuck out her tongue at her, and we all laughed. "It could happen," Jessica said.

"In your dreams," Ellen teased her.

"Really, you guys, I don't think we have anything to worry about," I said. "We should be glad that we're such good friends. And I have to say, I don't really sympathize with Janet. Even if this Chris guy was really cute, she shouldn't have tried to go after him when she knew her friend liked him."

"Yeah," Ellen said. "It's not exactly the way you want to treat your friends."

"I have an idea," Lila said. "Let's make that part of the Unicorn pledge."

"What pledge? We don't have one," I pointed out.

"Not yet, but we could," Lila said. "Let's make one up. Let's all promise that we'll never let romance get in the way of *our* friendship. Friends come first, guys come second. OK?" She looked around the table at everyone.

Ellen nodded quickly in agreement, but Jessica didn't look so sure. And at that moment, I felt a little funny about pledging something like that. I mean, I believed in it, in theory, but when it came to *pledging* . . . Well, pledges were just so . . . official. Suddenly, I pictured some terrific guy coming along. . . . But then, friends were more important, in the long run. Wasn't that what I'd just said?

I cleared my throat and smiled at Lila.

"Definitely." I glanced at Jessica. "What about you?"

Jessica ran her fingers through her hair. "Oh, yeah, of course," she said quickly. "It goes without saying, doesn't it? Then again, let's not forget another important factor."

"What other important factor?" Ellen asked.

Jessica smiled slyly. "You know what they say. All's fair in love and war, right?"

I couldn't help grinning. "That's what they say."

"And who are we to argue?" Jessica replied with a shrug.

Lila groaned in disgust. "You guys, you can't pledge to put your friends first and then say it's OK to go after guys they like at the same time," she complained.

"Yeah, that's contra- . . . counter- . . ." Ellen stammered.

"It's totally fine," Jessica declared. "As long as no one gets hurt."

"Right," I said. "Look, there's no way I'd ever intentionally hurt any of you guys. But things happen, you know?"

Lila frowned. "Some friends you are."

"Lila, we're only spending the whole weekend at a dude ranch, thanks to Kimberly," Jessica said. "I think she's proved what a good friend she is."

"After this weekend, we're going to be even better friends," I said, smiling at everybody. "My mother says there's nothing like going on a trip together to cement a friendship."

"We're going to have a blast," Ellen declared. "Only I have to ask you guys a favor. No fighting, OK? My mom and dad have been arguing all week, and it's been driving me crazy. I can't wait to get out of our house. So promise me you guys won't argue all weekend, because if you do, I might as well just stay home and—"

"Relax, Ellen," I told her, putting my hand on her arm. "Nobody's going to argue. We're practically going to a five-star resort. What could we possibly have to argue about?"

"Oh, I don't know," Jessica said, buffing her fingernails on the edge of her shirt. "How about who gets to clean out the horses' stalls when we're done riding for the day?"

"That's 'muck out,'" I said.

"Whatever it is, I'm not doing it!" Lila declared. "Friendship only goes *so far*."

# Three

"Tortilla chips?"

"Check."

"Chocolate peanut butter brownies?"

"Check."

"Riding clothes?"

"What do you think I am, stupid?" Ellen asked.

"Portable CD player?"

Jessica patted her duffel bag. "Right here."

"OK, Dad," I said. "Hit the freeway!"

Ellen let out a whoop as we pulled out of the Sweet Valley Middle School parking lot, and we waved at some people we knew who were starting to walk home from school. "Everyone looks so bored!" Ellen commented.

"Of course they are," Lila said. "They're not spending the weekend with us!" She and Jessica were sitting in the minivan's middle seat, and they were turned around, facing me, Mandy, and Ellen in the backseat.

"This is going to be great," Jessica said. Then she leaned closer and lowered her voice. "Two whole days without any parents around!"

"Don't get too excited," I told her. "We do have a chaperon up there."

"Yeah, but we can stay up as long as we want and talk all night," Jessica said. "It'll be like the longest sleepover in history."

"Maybe we should have brought some coffee, if we're going to stay up all night," Mandy joked.

"Actually, I bet we'll be tired after riding all day," I predicted. "The horses are going to be incredibly beautiful, probably nicer than any I've ever ridden. My mom and dad went to this ranch about two years ago, and they told me about this horse named Kentucky King, who's supposedly an ex-champion and tears around the trails."

"Tears around the trails?" Mandy repeated, drumming her fingers against the armrest. "Really? Like, how fast?"

I examined her face, which was starting to look a little pale. "What's wrong?" I asked. "Aren't you looking forward to riding?"

Mandy cleared her throat. "Oh, sure. It's just that the last thing I need is to be riding the Kentucky Derby on some mountainside trail, on the edge of the cliff. I'm more the . . . relaxed, trotting kind of rider, you know? I like ambling along at a casual pace. That way I get the chance to observe nature, listen to the birds, stop and smell the roses, and all that."

"Me too," Ellen said. "I tried galloping once, and I nearly had a heart attack."

"Well, I love to ride fast." I sighed happily. "The faster the better. But don't worry, I'm sure they have horses for beginners, too." After all, I knew that not everyone was as experienced as I was. I just hoped my friends wouldn't fall *too* far behind. It could get kind of embarrassing, actually.

Jessica shrugged. "I don't care if they give me a mule. As long as it doesn't rain, I'll be happy just to be outside in the mountains."

"Hey, that reminds me," Mandy said, sitting up in her seat. "I hope it doesn't rain next weekend, because we're having a car wash to raise money for the day-care center."

"We?" I said.

"Me and the rest of the Angels," Mandy explained. "We just decided at lunch today."

"Oh." I tapped my fingers against the window. A car wash. How thrilling. I stared at the wheels of a huge truck as we passed it on the highway.

"Why a car wash?" Lila asked. "I mean, isn't that going to be kind of . . . well . . ."

"Soapy?" Mandy asked with a smile.

"Actually, *dirty* is what I was thinking," Lila said. "Not to mention disgusting, grimy, and—"

Mandy laughed. "I know, I know. It's not exactly glamorous, wearing sweats and scrubbing grease off people's BMWs, but we want to use the money for an entertainment fund for the kids. We can use what we make to take them to special events, like the circus that's coming next month.

"How much are you going to charge?" Ellen asked.

"Well . . . for your bike, I think a dollar would cover it," Mandy told her with a grin. "Drying not included. You'll have to ride it around until the seat stops squishing."

Ellen hit her on the arm. "No, really. How much? I'll get my parents to bring their car."

"I don't know—a dollar or two, I guess," Mandy said.

"That sounds like a great idea," Jessica said. "Since it's cheap, I bet you'll get a lot of business."

"Yeah, but that might be a problem," Lila said. "I mean, there are only five of you, right?"

"Yeah . . ." Mandy said slowly.

"Well, when my dad takes our car to that deluxe car wash over by the mall—you know, the Octopus? They use, like, six people per car. Or is it eight? Anyway, even if you guys all work on each car, you won't be as fast as those guys, so then there'll be a huge line. Or just two of you could work on each car and you could do more cars, but then you might not do as good a job, and—"

"What is this, a math problem?" Mandy broke in, laughing.

"Yeah, you're staiting to scare me, Lila," Ellen added. "Don't ask me how many cars per hour the Octopus can do and how many the Angels can do if they each—"

"Wait a minute!" Mandy looked at me, then Ellen, then Lila and Jessica. A huge smile spread across her face. "I have a great idea! It's perfect. It's brilliant. The Unicorns *plus* the Angels!"

"What?" I asked. I didn't like the look on Mandy's face—not one bit. "You're not suggesting that we *help*, are you?"

Mandy shrugged. "Sure, why not? It'd be twice as many people, and we could wash twice as many cars."

"And raise twice as much money," Ellen chimed in.

"Nine people—an octopus plus one!" Jessica exclaimed. "Sounds great!"

"Forget it!" I cried.

Everyone looked at me as if I'd suddenly grown two heads. Even my *dad* turned around. I guess I'd said that kind of loud. OK, maybe I was overreacting a little bit, but I had my reasons. Good reasons. And my friends should have known how I felt by now. Did I really need to go over everything *again*?

"Look, I know it's not the most fun way to spend your Saturday, Kimberly, but it's for a great cause," Mandy argued.

"Maybe it is, but for your information, we can come up with plenty of great causes on our own." I sniffed. "There's no way the Unicorns are going to help the Angels. If we want to do something for charity, we will—without any help from you. Really, the whole idea's ridiculous. We're two separate clubs!"

"It was just a suggestion," Mandy said quietly.

"Well, don't even think about us working as a team, even if it is for the kids," I said.

"OK, OK," Jessica said. "Let's not fight about it. We have bigger problems to deal with."

"Such as?" I asked, raising one eyebrow.

"Whoever shares a room with Lila can forget about closet space," Jessica said, pointing to the stack of flowered designer luggage behind the backseat.

"Look who's talking!" Lila said. "You brought almost as much stuff, plus your CD player and all those CDs."

I smiled, glad we'd changed the subject. "I don't know if dude ranches *have* closets," I said. "Don't cowboys pretty much wear the same thing every day? Worn-out blue jeans, plaid shirt . . ."

"Are you telling me I'll be living out of a suitcase all weekend?" Lila looked horrified.

"No, more like *in* one," Mandy teased her. "With all the stuff you brought, I don't think you'll even be able to fit in your room!" We all laughed.

Lila just tossed her hair. "I'm sure the valet can find room for my stuff," she said.

"Valet?" I repeated, giggling. "Lila, you're not expecting valets and maids and room service, are you?"

"It's a dude ranch, not the end of civilization," Lila said.

"Yeah, but I showed you those pictures, remember?" I asked her. "The Sunset Dude Ranch is for people who like roughing it."

"Hey, I can rough it as well as the next person," Lila said, adjusting the seat belt on her lap.

"Oh, of course you can." Jessica looked at me and winked. "That is, if roughing it means going without maid service for a whole hour."

"For your information, I do not have a personal maid twenty-four hours a day," Lila said, as if it were the most ridiculous thing she'd ever heard.

"Of course not," Ellen teased. "You have to sleep at least eight hours, don't you?"

Then we all started giggling—even Lila.

"Let me get this straight. I'm supposed to sleep on *this*?" Lila poked the straw-filled mattress, which rustled. "I'd have better luck sleeping outside on the ground!"

"You're welcome to try that, too, but we do have the occasional rattlesnake," Mrs. Margot, Sunset Dude Ranch's director, told her. She had shown us around the ranch, the cabins that families stay in, and the stables and riding rings. My father had gone on the tour, too, so he could point out some of his favorite things to me, including the horse he'd ridden.

After leading us through the main lodge, Mrs. Margot had taken us upstairs to see our accommodations: a suite of two sparsely furnished connecting bedrooms. We had all started unpacking our stuff, except Lila, who was probably waiting for one of us to offer to be her valet for the weekend.

Lila stared at Mrs. Margot. "What? There are rattlesnakes here? Where? They don't come inside, do they?" She put one foot up on the bed, as if she was about to climb onto it and stand there.

I would have laughed at her if I hadn't been kind of freaked out myself. I don't like snakes, either—or mice, or spiders, or anything that can crawl on me. Except maybe a koala bear.

"Don't worry, I'm sure I haven't seen one in years," Mrs. Margot assured all of us. "Well, months, anyway. But I think you'll find these beds comfortable after a day on the trail."

"They look great to me," I said, smiling politely. I wanted to start out on the right foot with Mrs. Margot, in case we got too loud or something one night.

"A good pillow's all I need," Mandy added.

"Are there rattlesnakes on the trail?" Lila wondered, looking anxiously out the window.

"I'm sure you girls will be very comfortable," my father said. He smiled at Mrs. Margot. "This place is just as charming as I remember it."

"It's totally charming," Mandy said, checking out an old silver-framed photo of a cowboy on the redwood log-cabin-style wall. "In fact, I think I'll stick around inside the lodge for the entire weekend, listening to Patsy Cline tapes. There's a lot of history here, you know?"

"Yeah, right." Jessica laughed. "I'm sure we just drove a hundred miles so we could sit inside learning when the logs were cut to make the cabins."

"I can tell you more about this place later, if you like," Mrs. Margot offered politely.

"That would be great," Mandy said. "I for one am very interested in hearing about this place's history. So there."

"I guess we forgot you're such a scholar," Lila said, teasing her.

"Kimberly, I'll say good-bye for now, and leave you girls to unpack while I settle up with Mrs. Margot downstairs," my father said. We gave each other a kiss, and hugged. "I'll be here Sunday to get you. Now, have fun, but don't do anything against the rules—all right?" He smiled at everyone.

Jessica smiled back innocently. "Never even crossed my mind."

"Right, Jessica." My father nodded knowingly. "Well, call me if you need anything," he said, hugging me again.

"OK. Bye, Dad." I blushed, feeling kind of embarrassed. He gets all sappy whenever I'm going away for the weekend.

As he and Mrs. Margot headed down the hall, I turned to my friends. "So who's sleeping where?" I asked.

"Jessica and I want this room," Lila declared.

"I'll stay in here with Jessica and Lila," Mandy said to me. "That leaves you and Ellen next door, I guess. Is that OK with you guys?"

"Perfect," I said happily. I didn't want to say anything, but I'd kind of wanted the two-bed room instead of the three-bed one. I liked my space, you know?

Jessica sat down on a bed by the window and started unpacking her compact discs. "Kimberly, this place is so cool. It's just like I pictured it."

"Wish I could say the same," Lila said wryly. "How is a person expected to sleep with only one lumpy pillow?"

Gazing out the window, Mandy gasped. "Look! There really is an incredible sunset at this place."

I looked out the window over Jessica's bed. The sun was glowing orange-red as it started to sink behind the mountains.

"Do you see any cute cowboys out there?" I asked Mandy, joining her at the window.

"Nah. They're probably in their room, just like us," Mandy said, rubbing at a spot on the window. "Polishing their spurs or something."

"Probably," I said. I hoped we'd meet some boys later—it would make the whole weekend even more fun.

"I love all the redwood in here," Lila said, as she hung up some clothes in the closet.

"And I love this quilt." Jessica smoothed the antique quilt made of a red-and-blue bandanna-like fabric. She leaned back on the bed and put her hands behind her head on the pillow. "This is the life."

"If we had room service, it would be," Lila said, pushing at a dresser drawer. "Jessica, I can't fit any of my stuff in here—you took all the drawers!"

"I did not," Jessica protested.

"Actually, I took the bottom one," Mandy admitted.

"OK, then—Jessica, you took three out of four," Lila said. "Where am I supposed to put my clothes?"

"I don't know." Jessica shrugged. "It's not my problem that you overpacked."

"*I* overpacked? What about you?" Lila cried. "You should ask Mrs. Margot if you can have your own room! Maybe then I'd have enough space to put my things."

"If I'm such a horrible roommate, why don't you ask her for a private room for yourself? I don't see anyone else around here complaining about me," Jessica said smugly.

"Well, it's only a matter of time!" Lila said.

Ellen jumped up off her bed. "Time out, you guys. We just got here, and already you're fighting? I told you at lunch yesterday, I really don't want to hear any more arguments, OK?"

"Relax, Ellen. We can work something out," I said. "Jessica, maybe you could clear out one of those drawers for Lila?"

"No way." Jessica folded her arms. "I got them first."

"Oh, nice attitude." Lila threw up her hands. "Have you ever heard of being considerate?"

"Not from you, that's for sure," Jessica retorted.

"Look, you guys. There's a simple solution to this little . . . wardrobe problem," Mandy said. "Jessica, you move into the other room with Kimberly, and Ellen will move in here. Is that OK with you, Ellen?"

"Why should I move my stuff? I unpacked already," Jessica protested.

"Because I said a million times that I want this bed by the picture window," Lila said. "If you'd bothered to listen to me, you'd know!"

"And so Lila, Ellen, and I will be in here, and Jessica—and all her *stuff*—and Kimberly will be next door. Is that *OK* with everyone?" Mandy said, sounding more stern this time.

"Oh, all right," Jessica grumbled, looking sheepish as she shuffled over to the dresser.

"It sounds fine to me," I said, smiling at Mandy. I was glad she was so good at taking control of these situations; Lila and Jessica's arguing was starting to give me a headache.

I turned to Ellen and shrugged. "See you, roomie."

She smiled. "Yeah, see you. It's been fun." She went into the other room and grabbed her things, while Jessica started yanking clothes out of the dresser drawers and flinging them past her into the room.

"Hope you like living in a hurricane," Lila commented to me under her breath. "If I were you I'd get in there now and claim at least *one* hanger."

"It's OK," I said. "My riding clothes don't take

up that much room." Unlike my friends, I was here to *ride*, not to put on a fashion show.

"So when do we get to meet all the boys?" Ellen asked a few minutes later, flopping onto Lila's bed. We were all hanging out and listening to one of Jessica's CDs, as though nothing had ever happened between Jessica and Lila.

"Dinner, I guess," I told her, adjusting a stray lock of hair that had come out of my barrette. "I hope there are at least a couple worth looking at."

"There have to be," Jessica declared. "I mean, this is a dude ranch."

"Yeah, don't they practically promise dudes in the brochure?" Mandy skimmed the list of rules and regulations on the back of the suite's door.

Suddenly, there was a loud knock at the door, and Mandy jumped.

"Maybe that's the dudes!" Jessica said excitedly.

Mandy's eyebrows shot up. "Who is it?" she asked nervously.

"It's me!" Mrs. Margot said cheerfully. She opened the door a crack. "Girls, you're welcome to come downstairs for dinner now. We eat home-style here, nothing fancy. You'll get a chance to meet some of the other guests."

"Great," Jessica said, smiling mischievously.

I grinned, too. *Other guests*, of course, meant *cute boys*.

"Oh, and you'll also be able to meet my son, Herbert," Mrs. Margot continued.

"Herbert?" Ellen said with surprise.

"Yes," Mrs. Margot said slowly. "Why?"

Ellen shrugged, her face turning pink. "Oh, it's just—I—I've never met anyone named Herbert. Personally, that is."

"Actually, I think my parents have a friend named Herbert," I said, trying not to laugh. *Actually, it's my grandmother's friend,* I wanted to say. *And he's about eighty-five years old!*

"Perhaps it is a bit unusual," Mrs. Margot said. "Well, anyhow, Herbert will be your riding instructor. He's a high school junior, and he helps out here on weekends. I think you'll like Herbert. Of course, I may be biased, but he's a very nice young man. See you at dinner!"

"OK, uh, we'll be right down," Jessica told Mrs. Margot, obviously trying not to crack up laughing.

"Yeah, tell Herbert we're looking forward to meeting him," I added with a smile.

"Will do," Mrs. Margot said, closing the door.

We all burst out laughing as soon as she was gone. "Now, this I have to see!" I said. "A riding instructor named Herbert? What are we, traveling back in time or something?"

"Hey, Herbert might be really cute, for all we know," Mandy said. "Maybe his gorgeous cousin *Elmer* will join us for dinner."

\*        \*        \*

The second we walked into the dining room, my hopes that we'd meet a group of five cute boys shriveled to nothing. All I saw in the way of boys were some six-year-old twins running around, knocking silverware off the tables.

"Justin, Jake—you boys calm down right now," their mother said sternly.

The two long picnic tables in the dining room were occupied by older couples, some middle-aged, some more elderly, and a couple of families with young children.

I looked at my friends' disappointed faces. "So much for finding any romance this weekend," I mumbled.

Lila sighed. "The words *total washout* come to mind."

"Oh, well," Ellen said, as we slid onto bench seats at the end of one of the tables. "I guess you can't have everything."

I took a deep breath, determined not to let this little disappointment ruin our weekend. "We'll have fun anyway."

"Yeah, maybe we can ride the horses over to another dude ranch where there are some boys," Jessica said, gazing around the large room.

"You guys are so boy-crazy!" Mandy said with a laugh. "Don't you think about anything else?"

"Of course we do," Lila said.

"Yeah. Clothes, music . . . shopping for clothes and music," Jessica joked. "I know that's what Elizabeth thinks we think about anyway."

"Well, I can't say I'd ever turn down the chance to shop," Mandy said with a smile.

"Aha!" I cried. "That proves it! You are more a Unicorn than an Angel."

"That's not exactly true," Mandy protested. "I mean, just because I—"

"Attention, everyone!" Mrs. Margot rang a large bell over by the door, interrupting her. "Good evening!"

"Good evening," several guests replied cheerfully.

"Howdy," Mandy said. She giggled.

Mrs. Margot smiled. "I know you all are probably hungry, but before we eat, I've got a couple of Sunset Dude Ranch traditions for you. First, I'd like to welcome all of our new guests to the ranch." She started clapping, and everyone joined in. I applauded as loudly as I could.

"Second," Mrs. Margot continued once the noise had died down, "my son always sings a few nice, down-home country-western songs to welcome all the weekend guests."

"Herbert the trail guide singing country and western?" Ellen whispered, giggling.

"Down-home? What does *that* mean?" I asked in a quiet voice.

"I think it means downright awful," Lila said, looking doubtful.

"Yeah. Don't expect Johnny Buck," Jessica said, rolling her eyes, as the lights in the dining room dimmed.

Mrs. Margot turned on a small lamp next to a bar stool. "Now, everyone, if you'll join me in welcoming . . . the future star of Nashville . . . Herbert Margot!" she announced.

"I can't believe he's actually going to sit here and sing for us," I said, already feeling a little embarrassed for him as I watched the door for his entrance. "This Herbert must be a real . . . a real . . ."

Suddenly, the words died on my tongue. I blinked, as the most gorgeous guy I had ever seen in my entire life walked into the room, wearing cowboy boots and carrying a guitar.

"A real *hunk*," I whispered when I had finally gotten my voice back. I gazed up at Herbert, my eyes wide with amazement. A *total* and complete hunk!

# Four

One thing was sure: Herbert's looks definitely made up for his old-fashioned name. He had deep-blue eyes and sandy-brown hair that peeked out beneath his battered cowboy hat. He had the cheekbones of a model. He was tall with faded jeans and a very soft-looking plaid flannel shirt.

Need I say anything more?

If Herbert had just sat there under that little lamp all night, like the plants in my mother's greenhouse, it would have been enough.

But he didn't just sit there. He started *singing*. And he had the most incredible, deep, gorgeous voice I'd ever heard.

That's when I went over the edge: I didn't just have a crush on him. I was totally, passionately in love with him.

"And that's why I'll always love you . . ." Herbert finished the song, plucking out a few last notes on his guitar. Then he pushed his cowboy hat up on his head and looked out at the audience. Not just at the audience—right at me!

My heart started pounding so fast, I thought I was going to pass out, right there in the dining room of a dude ranch. But I knew that wouldn't impress a cowboy like Herbert, so I tried to look cool and collected as I smiled back at him and applauded.

"Hello, and welcome to the Sunset Dude Ranch," he said. "It's great to see y'all here tonight."

*Likewise, I'm sure,* I thought, gazing into his eyes.

"I'd like to play just one more song, and then we can get down to what's known among cowboys as chow," Herbert said. "I wouldn't want to be accused of making anyone go hungry. If I hear anyone's stomach growling out there, I'll quit a few stanzas early, all right?"

I realized that everyone around me was laughing. But I couldn't. I was too busy concentrating on Herbert's face, my heart pounding with anticipation. He started strumming his acoustic guitar, and I felt a chill go down my spine. I don't know why, but I just had a feeling that this was going to be one of those incredibly important moments in my life, one that I'd never forget and that might change everything.

After playing a few bars of music on his guitar, Herbert started to sing again. His voice was as good as any I'd ever heard on the radio. The first line was something like, "Honey, you promised you'd never leave me . . ."

It was all I could do to restrain myself from jumping up and yelling, "I know I've only known you for five minutes, but I'll never leave you, Herbert!"

Jessica poked me. "He's pretty good, you know?"

"Pretty good?" I scoffed. More like great, fantastic, amazing . . . "Jessica, he's incredible," I said. Of course, I couldn't expect everyone to see that. As Herbert glanced over at me again, my heart beat double-time. I could already feel that Herbert and I had a special connection.

Only I knew just how wonderful a singer—and person—Herbert really was.

Funny. I'd been absolutely starving a few minutes ago. Now I could care less about dinner. I wanted Herbert to sing all night!

"I never thought I'd say this, but what a great song!" Lila took a sip of water as she stared straight at where Herbert was standing, a glazed expression on her face. We'd all applauded fiercely at the end of his song. That four minutes was better than any two-hour Johnny Buck concert I'd ever been to.

I nodded, looking at Herbert while he talked to his mother and laughed. He even *laughed* gorgeously. "The best," I said, my eyes on Herbert.

"Unbelievable," Ellen added.

"Grammy-winning, as far as I'm concerned," Mandy said.

I sighed. "You know, you're right—he's as good as anyone on the radio, or TV, or . . ." *The planet.* If Herbert really wanted to make it in Nashville, he wouldn't have any problems. I, for one, would be the first in line to buy his CD. Or ten of them, because I'd probably wear them out by listening to them so much.

And it wasn't just his voice, it was all of him— even the rip on the knee of his faded blue jeans was perfectly placed. I could just picture him, gallantly hopping over a fence and catching his knee on the barbed wire. He probably even had a perfect *scar.*

I didn't know how Mrs. Margot expected us to eat after a life-changing experience like that, but the waiters brought out huge dishes of mashed potatoes and beans and a platter of sliced roast beef and started passing them down our table. I grabbed a roll from the basket on the table and absentmindedly started buttering it, just so I had something to do. Nervous energy, I guess. About ten million kilowatts of it.

"Kimberly—stop!" Ellen cried, grabbing my hand.

I looked down at my hand, which was covered with butter. I smiled sheepishly and put the knife down on my plate, then quickly rubbed the butter off my hand with a napkin. I giggled. When I start getting more spacey than Ellen, then you know it's time to worry about me.

"Look out, everyone. He's coming this way," Lila said. She daintily dabbed the corners of her mouth with a napkin.

"Who? Herbert?" I whispered, afraid that if I glanced over my shoulder, I might look too obvious.

"No—Spiderman," Lila said. "Of course it's Herbert."

I cleared my throat and tried to look beautiful. I didn't want to be caught brushing my hair or putting on fresh lip gloss or anything—that would be too tacky. So I just assumed a casual, this-is-no-big-deal attitude, even though my heart was pounding just thinking about meeting him.

*Stay cool. Don't worry. He already thinks you're cute,* I told myself. Or else why would he have stared at me during the whole, entire performance? He obviously wanted to talk to me.

"I knew he'd come over here to meet me. Did you see him looking into my eyes when he was singing?" Jessica asked in a dreamy voice.

I felt as if I was going to fall backward off the bench I was sitting on. Herbert looking into *Jessica's* eyes when he was singing? Hardly! If he'd glanced her way once, I'd be surprised. He'd been staring at *me* the whole time, and she knew it.

But before I could say anything, I sensed someone standing behind me. "Hi, there. You must be the Haver group," Herbert said, his voice sounding even lower up close. "My mother told me about you."

"She did?" I turned around, looked up at Herbert—he was at least six feet tall—and smiled. "I mean, of course she did. She told us all about you, too."

"Uh-oh," Herbert said, glancing over his shoulder at Mrs. Margot. "Nothing bad, I hope?" He raised one eyebrow.

"Not at all. I'm Kimberly Haver. And that song was absolutely terrific." I couldn't believe how smooth I sounded. I was so nervous, I had been afraid I'd stammer every word.

"Nice to meet you, Kimberly." Herbert grinned and held out his hand. I shook it, feeling a tingle traveling up my spine. Shaking hands wasn't normally something I did, but this felt wonderful, almost like we were holding hands. "And who are your friends?" He released my hand.

*Never mind about them!* I felt like saying. His eyes were an intense shade of blue, like the sky on a clear day in the country, or, if you're from the city, like pool water with too much chlorine. But they were even more beautiful than that. Trust me.

"This is the Unicorn Club," I started to explain to Herbert. "I'm the president. And these are—"

"I'm Jessica." Interrupting me, Jessica tossed her hair back and smiled at him. "And this is Mandy, Lila, and Ellen," she added in a rush, like it was all one long name.

Herbert nodded. "Well, are you guys ready to do some serious riding tomorrow? My mother tells me I'm going to be your trail guide and official riding instructor."

My heart leaped. This weekend was getting better and better. "We're definitely ready," I said, moving a little closer to him. "In fact, I've been looking forward to this trip for weeks."

"You girls must love horses an awful lot to spend your weekend at a dude ranch," Herbert said. "You could be at a football game, or a school dance—"

"No, right here is exactly where we want to be," Jessica told him.

"Yeah, this place is gorgeous," Mandy added, gazing up at Herbert. "Ab . . . solutely gorgeous."

"Lots of things we didn't really expect," Lila said, beaming.

"You've been pleasantly surprised, I hope?" Herbert asked.

Pleasantly surprised wasn't quite how I would have put it. More like bowled over, absolutely astonished, and completely wrecked. If a freight train had hit me, it would have had less impact.

"Oh, yes," Jessica said to him, looking at him with big, sparkling eyes.

I frowned. I was getting a little annoyed at everyone else for talking to Herbert when he had come over to talk to me in the first place. "You know what, Herbert?" I said. "It's even nicer here than I ever imagined. And we haven't even gone riding yet, which personally I can't wait for." I looked up at him and smiled. "I've been riding for years."

"An old pro?" Herbert asked, his blue eyes twinkly.

"Well, I guess you could say that," I said modestly. "But my friends are kind of . . . well, beginners," I said in a quiet voice. "I'm the one who planned this trip, and some of them are kind of like . . . you know, fish out of water, I guess." I wrinkled my nose. "You know."

"Don't worry, Kimberly, they'll be old ranch hands by the end of tomorrow," Herbert said. "I'll see to it."

I nodded. "Thanks. And if you could help me brush up on a couple of skills, too? That would be awesome."

"Be glad to. Now, if you all just make sure to meet me at the stables bright and early tomorrow morning, we're going to have a great day riding," Herbert said. "I'd better move on to meet some more folks. See you tomorrow, then?"

"We'll be there," Lila said.

"With spurs on," Mandy joked.

Grinning, Herbert tipped the brim of his hat and then suddenly he was gone. I felt my pulse sink back into some kind of normal range.

"Do you think if we asked really nicely, he'd sing an encore?" Ellen asked.

"Please don't," Jessica said. "Besides, I'm sure he'll sing again before we leave." She put two big slices of roast beef on her plate. "Check out this food! I can't wait to send Elizabeth a postcard! She won't believe it. I only got here an hour ago, and I feel like I never want to leave."

Everyone started digging into dinner. I lifted a forkful of potatoes and gravy to my mouth, and chewed and swallowed without even tasting it. I wasn't hungry anymore. I was too busy thinking about how impressed Herbert was going to be when he saw me riding the next morning. He wouldn't even notice anyone else in our group, that's how good I was. I don't mean to brag—it's just that I've had tons of lessons and I've spent more hours on horses than everyone else combined.

I knew what would happen. Herbert and I would probably leave everyone behind, dawdling down a dirt road, while we raced up into the mountains along dusty trails.

Just me and Herbert . . . Herbert and me . . . It was going to be wonderful.

"I'm so glad I moved in here with you," Jessica said, climbing into her bed across the room from me later that night. "There's tons of room, and I don't have to listen to Lila complaining about my stuff."

I punched the pillow on my bed behind me and leaned back against it. Jessica and Lila's argument seemed incredibly far off. Years ago. Ever since I'd met Herbert, he was all I could think about. There was Before Herbert, and there was After Herbert.

"Aren't you tired?" Jessica said. "I'm exhausted. We didn't even *do* anything yet, and it's only, like, eleven. I thought we were going to stay up all night and talk and stuff."

"We were," I said. "But I think it's more impor-tant to get a good night's sleep so we're ready for

tomorrow." So we're ready for Herbert, more specifi-
cally. The last thing I planned on doing was falling
asleep at the reins. If there was ever a night when I
was hoping for "beauty sleep," this was it. "The only
problem is, I'm not tired. I don't know if I'm going to
be able to sleep at all, actually," I told Jessica.

"Why? Is your bed uncomfortable?" she asked.
"I mean, this isn't the softest thing I've ever slept
on, but I'm so tired, I don't even care."

"No, it's not the mattress," I confessed. "It's . . .
being here."

Jessica sat up in bed and leaned her back
against the wall. "Kind of exciting to be away from
home, huh?"

"Yeah," I sighed. "But that's only half of it."

"What's the other half?" Jessica seemed confused. "Do you have insomnia or something?"

"In a way," I said. "I guess I'm just still so
wound up about meeting Herbert tonight."

"That was hours ago," Jessica commented. "Are
you still thinking about him? I mean, he is gorgeous, and he sings well, but we're not going to see
him for"—she glanced at the clock on the wall—"at
least ten hours."

"I know," I said. "It's just . . ." I paused. Should I
tell Jessica how I was really feeling? *Why not?* I decided. Everyone was going to know eventually.
Maybe she could give me some advice. I looked
over at her and felt my face turn pink. "Jessica,
don't laugh, but I think I'm in love."

She laughed. "Uh-huh."

"I'm serious!" I said with a frown. "And I told you not to laugh."

"Kimberly, I'm sorry, but you're always in love with somebody," Jessica said. "For a couple of days, anyway. Then you get sick of whoever it is and find someone else to have a crush on."

"This *isn't* a crush," I argued. As if it were anything even remotely close to a crush! "I know we only met Herbert tonight, but I'm telling you—he's the one for me. It's like fate, you know? I suggested we come up here this weekend, after I saw that ad in the magazine, and here's this guy who's perfect for me in every way—"

"Perfect for *you*?" Jessica exclaimed, looking baffled.

"Well, yeah," I said defensively.

"What makes you so sure? You don't even know him," Jessica said.

I sighed impatiently. She's never been logical in her entire life. Why was she starting now? "I can just tell, that's all," I said. "It's like a sixth sense. Jessica, you had to notice the way he kept staring at me when he was singing tonight. I mean, he was looking at me almost the whole time."

Jessica frowned. "I wouldn't say he was looking at you the *whole* time. Actually, I'm pretty sure he caught my eyes—"

"He might have looked around at everyone else at the table once or twice, you know, just to be polite. But he was staring at me the rest of the time," I insisted. "For, like, both songs."

"Whatever." Jessica didn't sound convinced. "Kimberly, you know, Herbert's a lot older than you. I don't think it's a good idea to really fall in love with him. You'd probably only get hurt, and that wouldn't be worth it, would it? Yeah, you'd better give up now."

"Give *up*?" I cried. "Yeah, right. So he's a little older—so what? Anyway, don't forget that I'm the oldest Unicorn now," I said. "Seventh grade and eleventh grade—there's not *that* much of a difference. Plus, we're almost in eighth grade. And everyone knows that girls mature faster than boys. *And* just last week my guidance counselor said I was very mature for my age, because I've had to move a couple of times."

"So what's your point?" Jessica asked.

Honestly! Jessica could be so dense sometimes. "I was just kind of thinking that if any of us are ready to go out with someone older like Herbert, it's me," I said.

"Look, I don't even know what we're talking about, anyway," Jessica said hurriedly. "Herbert's just our riding instructor, and that's that." She yawned, covering her mouth with her hand. "And I'm really tired. Can you turn out the light?"

I reached up and flicked the switch on the wall. "Good night," I told her, glad that this annoying conversation was ending.

"Good night," she said, disappearing beneath her quilt.

I sat up for a minute, thinking about how cute Herbert had looked, sitting under that lamp and strumming on the guitar. I could just imagine him sitting there and singing to me. Maybe he'd even write a song *about* me, if I was lucky.

I snuggled down under the covers. I was drifting off to sleep when I heard Jessica mumble something. Her voice was soft, but her words were unmistakable.

"All's fair in love and war, Kimberly."

# Five

*Clang! Clang! Clang!*

"What *is* that?" Jessica muttered, the antique quilt pulled up over her face.

I was awake for at least thirty seconds before I realized where we were. Then I figured out that the clanging noise was the huge bell downstairs, and someone was ringing it to wake us up—probably Mrs. Margot. I sniffed the air. The scent of frying eggs and baking cinnamon coffee cake was wafting through the room, and my stomach growled.

I looked out the window and saw the rolling hills, and then it hit me: I was going to meet Herbert in an hour and actually get to ride with him. As soon as he saw what a great rider I was, he'd know what I already knew: we belonged together. Talk about motivation to get out of bed!

I threw back the covers and practically sprinted to the bathroom the five of us were sharing. I wanted to make sure I had time to shower and look my absolute best by the time I went downstairs for breakfast. Just in case Herbert was there—and why wouldn't he be? He had to eat, too.

When I came back into our room ten minutes later, Jessica was standing in front of the mirror, brushing out her hair. She was wearing dark purple jeans, a long-sleeved white T-shirt, and black cowboy boots.

"Nice boots. When did you get those?" I asked her, as I went to the closet to get out my outfit for the day.

"They're Elizabeth's," Jessica said. "Aren't they great?"

I nodded and started pulling on my black jeans. "I can't wait to see the horses, can you?"

"The what?" Jessica asked.

"Horses?" I repeated.

"Oh, yeah," Jessica said. "Sure, that'll be great, too." She leaned closer to the mirror and started brushing some pink blush onto her cheeks.

"What do you mean, too? That's why we're here, remember?" I asked her, laughing.

"Well, there's also Herbert, of course," she said, leaning closer to the mirror and brushing an eyelash off her cheek.

I frowned. So. Jessica was thinking about Herbert, too. Just like me. And she was putting a lot of time into making herself look good, probably so that she could impress him.

Well, I couldn't let that get to me. I was the one who was going to get Herbert. If I had to compete with Jessica, fine. Did she think that one sort-of-cute outfit could compete with me riding at top speed with a guy who was a serious cowboy?

I dried my hair with the towel. "Well, Jessica, if I were you I'd start thinking about the horses. Do you even know how to get *on*to a horse?"

"Of course I do," Jessica said, turning around to face me. "It's easy."

"Uh-huh," I said with a laugh. "We'll see."

"You guys ready for chow?" Ellen called through the doorway between our rooms.

"Almost!" I called back.

"Come on, you cowpokes," Mandy said. She stood in the doorway, her thumbs crooked in the belt loops of her jeans. "Let's get a move on, little dogies."

"That's 'git along, little dogies,' " I corrected her.

"Who are you calling a dog." Jessica frowned.

"Just git along already and forget about that part," Mandy said. "If we're late for breakfast, we'll starve all day."

"OK, OK," I said. "I'm ready." I walked into the other room, and my eyes practically popped out of my head. Jessica wasn't the only one who'd dressed up to go riding!

I studied Mandy more carefully. She had on a

cool, retro outfit, which included a shirt with red piping and matching red cowboy boots. Ellen was wearing a new Hard Rock sweatshirt over black jeans and black riding boots, and Lila looked as though she'd just ordered everything from the Ride in Style catalogue. She was wearing her new alligator-skin boots with real silver spurs, a pair of blue jeans with leather patches on the thighs, and a bolo tie with a turquoise clasp over a crisp, pressed white blouse.

Was everyone thinking about impressing Herbert? What was their deal, anyway? As if someone like Herbert, a real cowboy, would be interested in someone who didn't know how to ride! They didn't stand a chance next to me. But I guess if they wanted to try, I couldn't stand in their way. In fact, it might almost be amusing.

"I'm going to see if they'll make me a cappuccino," Lila announced as soon as we settled down to breakfast.

I laughed. "Lila, I kind of doubt they have a cappuccino machine back there."

"Me too, but if they do, bring me a caffé latte," Jessica said, flipping her hair over her shoulder.

"Yeah," I said to tease Lila, as she started walking across the dining room, "and get me a couple of biscotti to go with that, OK? No, wait—I'll have an espresso, if—"

Suddenly, Lila tilted her foot back too far and one of her boot spurs caught on the rough wood floor. She tripped and went down with a thud. "Ow!" she cried.

For a moment, Jessica, Ellen, and I just looked at her in shock. "Are you OK?" Ellen asked at last.

"Somebody help me up already," Lila said, crawling onto her knees.

I couldn't help thinking that if Lila could barely make it across the lodge in her new boots, she was going to have a hard time down at the stables, with all the hay lying around. Not to mention getting onto her horse.

"Look—here comes Herbert," Jessica whispered loudly.

"What?" Lila jumped to her feet.

I glanced around the dining room. "Where?" I asked Jessica, as Lila took her seat across from me.

"Oh, I guess I must have confused him with someone else," Jessica said with a knowing smile. "Sorry." She shrugged.

Lila frowned at her. "Right. I bet you are."

"Nice trick," I said. "But you shouldn't kid around about serious stuff like that, you know."

"Where is Herbert, anyway?" Lila wondered. "Doesn't he eat?"

"He's probably down at the stables, getting our horses ready," I said. "He is our riding instructor, remember?"

Jessica sighed and put down the piece of toast in her hand. "How could I forget?"

I glared at her. She was really getting carried

away with this Herbert thing. It was funny, considering she knew how serious I felt about him. She ought to be finding her own riding instructor to have a crush on. Well, it would all be settled when we got down to the stables, I told myself. Then any sort of competition between me and Jessica would be officially over.

"Mandy, you'd better eat something," I said, pointing at the full plate of food in front of her. "We won't get lunch for a long time, and riding takes a lot of energy."

Mandy pushed her plate toward the center of the table. "I'm not hungry." She made a face and rubbed her stomach.

"I'm starving," Lila said, tearing a banana off the bunch in a bowl on the table. "It must be that mountain air thing."

"You're not feeling sick, are you?" I asked Mandy.

"Well . . . no, I feel OK," Mandy said.

"I wonder what we'll do today, where we'll go," Ellen said. "I hope my horse is nice."

"Of course he'll be nice," I said. "My parents said they have the best horses here. Mandy, sure you don't want half of this piece of coffee cake? I can't eat the whole thing."

"N-no." Mandy shook her head vigorously, her face turning a little paler. "Um, by the way, how big are these horses exactly?"

"Oh, probably fifteen, sixteen feet, tops," I said.

"That's in length, of course. Height—probably about six feet."

Mandy pushed her chair back from the table. "Uh, I have to, uh, go call home. I'm going to see if my mom can come pick me up."

"What?" Lila said. "What's wrong?"

A tear trickled down Mandy's cheek. "I . . . I can't stay here."

"What's wrong?" I asked her. "You're not homesick or anything, are you?"

"No, it's not that," Mandy said, biting her lip.

"Well, what is it, then?" Jessica asked. "I thought you loved it here."

"I do . . . I mean, I did. But the thing is— Look, I'm . . . afraid of horses," she blurted out. "More than afraid. Terrified."

"What?" I couldn't believe it. How could anyone be afraid of horses? "You're kidding."

Mandy shook her head and stood up. "There's no way I can go riding with you guys. I'd better go home right now."

# Six

"Mandy, I thought you loved riding," I said, completely baffled. "That's what you said, isn't it?"

"Yeah, you said you were like Dale Evans," Jessica reminded her. "What about all those horse books you have?"

Mandy sighed. "I don't *have* any horse books. I was just saying that." She wiped the tears off her face with a napkin.

Ellen looked confused. "Why would you even want to come if you hate horses so much?"

"I don't hate them," Mandy said. "I just—I don't know. I've never gone riding before, and the whole thing basically terrifies me. I mean, I don't even like big dogs. Horses are like . . . so much taller . . ." She looked as if she was about to pass out.

"Here, sit down." I patted the bench next to me

and gestured for her to get onto it. "And don't cry about it. I mean, if you're afraid of horses, no big deal. It's just like anything: if you want to get over it, you can."

Mandy sniffled. "That's what I thought. Only we're supposed to go riding in fifteen minutes, and I'm feeling sick to my stomach."

"You don't *have* to come along," Jessica told her. "If you want to hang out here and wait for us to get back, that's OK with me."

"Yeah," Ellen said. "Don't force yourself to do something that makes you feel sick."

"But you guys don't understand. I *have* to go," Mandy declared.

"Why?" I asked. "I mean, I hate snakes, and you don't see me forcing myself to have one for a pet or anything."

"I have to, because . . ." Mandy sniffled again. "Well, ever since I recovered from my cancer, I promised myself I'd seize every opportunity that came my way, that I'd never say no to any kind of adventure. So when you guys asked me to come along, I had to say yes. And I wanted to spend the weekend with you guys, I really did. Only I'm scared to death of horses, and the thought of riding makes me want to throw up."

"Well, don't do *that*," I told her. Yuck.

"Yeah, definitely don't," Lila added, giving Mandy a cautious look. "Or at least warn us first."

I hated for Mandy to sit there feeling sick about

something that was so easy. And fun, too, once you got good at it. I thought maybe I could help save her weekend, if she'd give it a chance. "I have an idea," I said. "You can ride with me! I know all about horses, and so you don't have anything to be afraid of."

Mandy looked up at me, smiling through her tears. "Really? You'd let me ride with you?"

"Of course," I said. "I'd be happy to help you." Coming to Mandy's rescue would be almost fun. I patted her on the arm. And if Herbert happened to find out that I'd helped one of my friends, and if he happened to think that was cool . . . well, that wouldn't exactly hurt my chances with him.

"But if you don't want to ride at all, you could hang out here and wait until we come back," Ellen suggested.

"No, I—I want to try it," Mandy said softly. "I mean, I want to get over my fear, if I can."

"Yeah, she should definitely at least try it," I said.

"Then let's hit the trail!" Jessica exclaimed. "Don't worry, Mandy—we'll *all* look after you. That's what being a Unicorn is all about."

Mandy smiled. "I should have known you guys would come through for me."

"We always have, and we always *will*," Lila declared. "Just don't talk about getting sick anymore, OK? I think I had one too many pieces of coffee cake." She rubbed her stomach.

"We'd better get going, if we're supposed to meet Herbert at the stables at eight. Here, take some food for the road. Maybe you'll feel like eating later," I told Mandy, wrapping a biscuit in a napkin and handing her a banana, too.

"Thanks!" Mandy said. We all got up and walked over to the door.

"Hey, look at this!" Lila exclaimed. Beside the door was a large bulletin board, with lists of all the guests, emergency phone numbers, and general information about the ranch. Lila pointed to a sheet marked "Daily Schedule of Events." "Saturday. Riding lessons, lunch, riding . . . and tonight, there's a big home-style barbecue and, get this, *line* dancing."

"Line dancing?" Ellen said. "What's that?"

"Some kind of country-western thing, right? I think I saw it on TV once," Jessica said.

"Kind of goofy, isn't it?" Lila asked.

Mandy shook her head. "Actually, it's pretty cool, especially when everyone's doing it."

"Do you actually know how?" I asked her.

"A little," Mandy said. "I can show you tonight, before dinner."

"Great," I said. "I'll help you ride, you'll help me dance. Deal?"

Mandy nodded, grinning at me. "Deal."

*Herbert was holding me close in his arms, and we were practically floating across the dance floor of the lodge. We turned in perfect syncopation, then moved to the other side. Everyone around us stopped dancing to watch us, they were so amazed at how perfect we looked together.*

*After our fourth or fifth dance, we wandered off to the fence around the corral. I sat up on the top rung of the fence, and Herbert grabbed his guitar from where he'd hidden it earlier, behind a fence post. Then he started singing, a private concert just for me, under the dark starry sky. . . .*

"Hey," Mandy said. "Look where you're walking!"

"Whoops—sorry," I sputtered. I had been so caught up in my daydream that I had crashed right into Mandy when she stopped walking.

"Kimberly, I'm not sure if I want to ride with you—you're acting like a real space cadet," she said, giving me a funny look. "What's up?"

"Oh, I was just . . . watching those riders over there." I pointed to what looked like some real cowboys, taming a bucking bronco in one of the rings to our right. "Aren't they amazing?"

"Yeah. Amazing," Mandy said weakly.

"Don't look," Ellen instructed her just as Herbert came around the corner of the stables and waved at us.

"No problem," Mandy muttered, gazing at him. "There are much more interesting things to look at."

I stared at her. Was she talking about Herbert? Did she have a crush on him or something? Her *and* Jessica?

"Good morning!" Herbert called to us. "Come on down, and let's get you saddled up."

Happily, I turned away from Mandy and walked toward him. He looked even more handsome in the

morning sunlight than he had the night before. He
was wearing faded, frayed jeans, a denim shirt with
metal snap buttons, and old brown cowboy boots.

*Take a deep breath, Kimberly,* I told myself. *If you
don't get your head out of the clouds, you're going to
make a fool of yourself.* I'm not usually the type to get
nervous around a boy. But Herbert wasn't just a boy.
He was . . . well, he was Herbert. It was different.

"Howdy, pardner," Jessica said, sauntering up to
him. "We had our chow and we're ready to ride."

Herbert grinned. "I like your attitude. Jessica,
right?"

She nodded. "Right! How did you remember?"

"Well, when you happen to get assigned to the
prettiest bunch of girls on the ranch, you make a
point to remember," Herbert said. "Good morning,
Kimberly."

My heart skipped a beat. He'd actually called
me pretty. "Hi, Herbert. What's up?" I brushed a
stray lock of hair off my forehead.

"It's a beautiful morning, isn't it?" Lila asked,
stepping closer to Herbert.

"Nice and sunny, just like we promised in the
brochure," Herbert replied. "Any of you girls ever
been to a dude ranch before?"

"Well, no, but I feel like I've been here my whole
life," Jessica said breathlessly before I could answer.
"You know what I really love, Herbert? Getting up
at the crack of dawn, and heading out to the corral,
just me and my horse and the rising sun—"

"Give me a break," Lila muttered. "You never get up before ten."

*No kidding*, I thought. Jessica only knew about corrals from old television shows like *Bonanza*. Some people will say anything to impress a guy.

"What did you say, Lila?" Herbert asked.

"Oh, nothing." Lila shook her head and bent down to pull a long piece of grass off her spurs.

"Those are some real fine boots," Herbert told her.

Lila looked as though he'd paid her the hugest compliment in the world. "Thanks—I got them in New Mexico."

Jessica cleared her throat. "Did I mention last night that I've been taking guitar lessons?"

"Since when?" I said. "Air guitar doesn't count."

"OK, girls, enough chatting," Herbert said cheerfully. "We've got some trails to hit, or your dude ranch vacation isn't going to be complete."

"It feels complete already," Lila sighed. "Did I tell you that my father owns a couple of ranches in Wyoming?"

"No. Where are they?" Herbert asked.

"Let's see. There's that one up near Laramie . . . and then—"

I turned and headed over to the horses lined up in the corral. Lila and Jessica could talk all they wanted to, and try to impress Herbert with their clothes and stories, but I knew the real way to his heart. "Herbert, which horse should I take?" I called over my shoulder as I climbed the fence around the corral and dropped down to the other side.

"Which one would you like?" Herbert asked me.

I looked at all of them. Each one was beautiful in its own way: there was a chestnut-colored mare with a white stripe down her nose, a white Appaloosa, a blue roan, and a few palominos. While I was studying them, the chestnut-colored mare swished her tail, hitting me on the arm. I smiled. She had to be giving me a sign! Besides, she looked young and full of energy, and she was definitely big and strong enough to carry both me and Mandy. "I'll take this one. What's her name?"

"That's Catalina. She's a four-year-old," Herbert said.

I picked a saddle off the fence and slung it over Catalina's back, hoping that Herbert was watching me and admiring my horse sense.

"Nice work!" Herbert said, watching me fastening the saddle girth as he walked through the gate into the corral.

I smiled. *So there,* I felt like saying to my friends, who were walking behind him.

When Herbert turned to latch the gate, Mandy was still standing on the other side. "Come on in, Mandy," he said. "Your feet might get a little dirty, but it's OK."

Mandy bit her lip. "Actually . . ."

"Mandy's never ridden before," I told Herbert. "She's not really sure what to do. She doesn't have a clue, actually."

"Oh, well, that's no problem," Herbert said. "Come on over, and I'll get you acquainted with your horse. After a couple of brief lessons, you'll be all set."

"I don't know," Mandy said hesitantly. "To tell you the truth, Herbert, I'm kind of afraid of horses. Maybe I should go back up to the lodge and help make lunch or something."

"Don't be ridiculous," Herbert said with a wave of his hand. "I'll take care of you."

"That's OK, Herbert," I said quickly. "I already told Mandy that she could ride with me."

"That's nice of you, Kimberly, but I think she'd be better off with me," Herbert said.

I felt a rush of panic. He wanted Mandy on *his* horse? "But—"

"Actually, I was about to offer to take her on my horse," Jessica said sweetly.

"I think Mandy should ride with me," Lila argued. "If anyone knows how to ride, it's me. I mean, my family does have its own stable. Come on, Mandy."

Herbert looked a bit uneasy as he glanced at each of us. "Listen, I'm sure you'd *all* do fine, but it's my job to look after all of you and make sure you have a good time. I'm the one who should monitor Mandy. Now, I'll just get everyone saddled up here, then I'll come over and pick you up, OK, Mandy? Don't be afraid—by the end of the day, I bet you'll be cantering all by yourself."

I felt the color drain from my face. I didn't like how the day was going so far—at all. Mandy was going to ride with Herbert, and to make matters worse, Jessica and Lila were still obviously competing for his attention.

There was only one thing to do. Show Herbert who the *real* rider was. I finished saddling Catalina, put my left foot in the stirrup, and pulled myself up onto her. I patted her neck and adjusted myself in the saddle, holding on to the reins. It felt great, sitting on such a tall horse and looking around at the gorgeous wide-open landscape.

Including Herbert, who tipped his hat to me. "Kimberly's way ahead of us, gang. Sitting tall in the saddle!"

I looked over at Jessica, who was still standing beside her horse, and smiled triumphantly. She frowned at me and started to get onto her horse.

"How does this thing go?" Lila asked, struggling with the saddle. She couldn't quite manage to lift it up onto the horse's back, and she kept hitting it against his side.

Before Herbert could reach over to help her, the horse got irritated and stomped the ground a few times with his back right leg.

"Agh!" Lila screamed, jumping backward and dropping the saddle.

"Did it kick you?" Ellen asked.

"What happened?" Jessica said, turning around.

Mandy and I were the only ones who had seen the whole thing, and we both started laughing. Lila wasn't hurt—she just needed a change of clothes . . . desperately!

"Agh! Euu!" Lila kept screaming. "Look at me!"

"Now, Lila, don't get upset," Herbert said. "It's just a little horse manure."

"A little horse manure? There's no such thing as a *little* manure!" Lila shrieked, staring at her jeans in horror. "I have to go change—wait for me!" She took off running, but she only made it as far as the corral gate before she caught her spurs on something and fell to the ground, face first. When she stood up, she had hay stuck in her hair.

I covered my mouth to keep from laughing. "Still getting used to your new boots, Lila?"

She turned to glare at me. "Very funny!" Then she leaned down, pulled off her cowboy boots, and went sprinting toward the lodge.

I grinned. I had a feeling Lila had just made an impression on Herbert that he'd *never* forget.


"Well, actually I just got back to California. My family had to move to Atlanta for a little while," I told Herbert as we waited for Lila. I was sitting on my horse, smoothing her mane.

"Georgia, huh? How did you like that?" Herbert asked.

"I loved it," I said. "Only I missed Sweet Valley a lot, especially all my friends." Though, at that moment, I wished all my friends had moved to Atlanta. Then Herbert and I could be alone. The way it should be.

"I've never been down south," Herbert said.

"Not on the East Coast, anyway. I've been to Mexico a couple of times."

"Don't you just *love* Mexico?" Jessica sidled up on the other side of Herbert.

"Yeah, it's nice," Herbert said. "But I guess I like this place better than anywhere else. Isn't that right, King?" He reached down and petted his horse's nose.

I sighed, watching his every move. "Yeah, I know what you mean. If I lived here I'd never leave either."

Lila ran up to us, panting, her face red. "I changed as quickly as I could." I had to admit, she looked fabulous. She was wearing a pair of new black riding boots, jodhpurs, and a red riding jacket. Maybe it pays to bring three suitcases, after all.

"Hope you didn't have to wait too long for me," she said, lifting her sunglasses off her eyes as she looked up at Herbert.

"No problem," Herbert said. "Just get on and we'll get started here."

Lila nodded and walked over to her horse, which Herbert had saddled for her. "OK, horse. That's the last time you do something like that."

"His name's Dusty," Herbert told her.

"*I'll* say." Lila brushed at his mane a few times, then climbed up onto the horse.

I stared at Herbert as he lifted Mandy up onto his saddle. In that instant, I wished I was the one who was afraid of horses. I would have given anything for Herbert to be wrapping his arms around *me*.

I looked over at her and smiled sweetly. "Mandy, are you sure you can handle this? I mean, if you want to wait in the lodge, we'd understand."

"No, I feel OK," Mandy said with a shrug. "Thanks for asking."

"Well . . . you feel OK now, but we haven't even moved out of the corral yet," I told her. "Wait until we're galloping up a cliff."

"What?" Mandy asked, panic flashing across her face.

Herbert patted her shoulder. "Don't worry, we'll start off slow," he told Mandy. "OK, everyone, let's go. Kimberly, why don't you go last?"

"Last?" I repeated, my heart sinking. Was he angry at me for trying to scare Mandy?

"Since you're the most experienced rider, you can keep an eye on the other girls," Herbert explained. "I know I can rely on you." He turned around and winked at me.

I practically leaped out of my saddle. "No problem!" I replied cheerfully. Herbert wasn't mad at me at all—he was paying me a compliment! Sure, he felt sorry for Mandy, but he *admired* me. He was going to *rely* on me. That was a lot different.

As far as I was concerned, he could rely on me from now to eternity.

# Seven

"How does that go? Yippie-yo-ho-ho?"

Herbert laughed. "No, not *quite*, Mandy."

"Yodel-ay-ee-hoo?" Mandy asked.

"I think that's on the Swiss dude ranches," Herbert said. "Maybe up in the Alps somewhere."

"Heidi's dude ranch, you mean?" Mandy joked.

I could hear Herbert laughing, like it was the funniest thing he'd ever heard. I'd always liked Mandy's sense of humor—until now. Now she was using it to charm Herbert, and it sounded as though they were having a great time together. I should have made sure she rode with me, just as we'd planned.

"Oh, I know—I've got it," Mandy declared. "Yippie-ay-kay-ai!"

"Well . . . close enough," Herbert told her. "You might want to practice a little bit before you go around shouting it at any rodeos."

"Me, at a rodeo?" Mandy giggled. "That'll be the day. I'd probably take up skydiving first."

"Maybe you could skydive onto a horse," Herbert said. "That'd be a great rodeo event."

"Yeah, and maybe you could skydive off Herbert's horse right now," I muttered under my breath. I pulled up on the reins and dropped back a little farther. I couldn't take any more. It was torture, sheer torture. There was Mandy, yakking it up and laughing her day away right behind Herbert. And here I was, picking up the end of the line, listening to the two of them while I watched their backs. Why didn't I just turn around and go back to the stables?

I took a deep breath. *Get a grip*, I told myself. I couldn't give up on Herbert just because he was nice enough to help Mandy get over her fear of riding. I couldn't really hold such a wonderful quality against him. He *had* said he was going to rely on me. And besides, we were passing through the most gorgeous country I'd ever seen, on wooden bridges over wide, clear streams, past sagebrush and tall pine trees. At least there was a good view.

We came out onto an open ridge, where we could see down to the ranch below. It looked so far away—I hadn't realized how far up we had been going. I could see for miles.

I was gazing out over the horizon when, directly in front of me, Jessica pulled up on the reins. Her horse stopped walking, and she waited for me to catch up to her. I stopped beside her. "What's up?"

She was practically glowering as she turned to face me. "Can you believe this?" she asked.

"Believe . . . what?" I replied.

"That!" she said, pointing ahead.

I had a feeling she wasn't talking about the gorgeous canyon scenery. "You mean Mandy?" I asked.

"Boy, do I," she said. "Can you believe the way she's joking around with Herbert, and talking to him like they're the only ones out here, like we don't even exist, like there aren't four horses behind them, like—"

"I know, I know," I interrupted. I was afraid Jessica was going to hyperventilate. "It's annoying, all right."

"Yeah," Jessica said. "And the whole thing seems pretty suspicious to me. How come her so-called horse phobia didn't emerge until *after* we'd all seen Herbert? She could have mentioned it before, don't you think? But she didn't, and I know why. This way she gets Herbert all to herself. It's not fair!"

"What are you saying? Do you mean she made the whole thing up?" I asked.

"Look at her!" Jessica cried. "Does that *look* like someone who's afraid of horses?"

"She doesn't seem very nervous or anything," I observed. "I mean, she's not even biting her nails, and she always does that."

"Kimberly, we're talking about the fastest recovery in history," Jessica insisted. "I'm telling you, she had to have been faking it."

"Maybe you're right." I had to admit—even

though Mandy had seemed genuinely upset that morning at breakfast, Jessica did have a point. Mandy had acted so scared that Herbert *had* to offer to take her on his horse, and then he had to look after her during our entire trail ride, just to make sure she was doing OK. "That seems like a lot of trouble to go through just to ride with Herbert, though."

"Yeah, well, not if you consider that she's in love with him," Jessica muttered.

"*She's* in love with him?" I repeated, my face heating up. "But *I'm* in—"

"Girls?" Herbert called back to us. Everyone had kept riding, while Jessica and I were stopped for a second, and now we were way behind. "Everything OK?"

"Everything's great!" I called back, smiling and waving at Herbert. *Except for the fact that Mandy's trying to steal you away from me!* I nudged my horse with the stirrups, and Jessica and I headed forward to catch up with Herbert.

"Yeah, everything's wonderful," Jessica muttered. "Just wonderful."

"You're not tired, are you?" Herbert asked. "We could all stop and take a break."

"No, we're not tired at all," Jessica told him.

"Yeah, we just wanted to check out the view for a second," I added. Only the view I really wanted to check out was right in front of me now: Herbert's face.

"It's really pretty, isn't it?" Ellen sighed.

Lila smiled at Herbert. "I love riding out here."

"Well, we'll stop in about an hour for lunch."

Herbert patted the saddlebags behind him. "I know a real nice spot. Sound good?"

"It sounds perfect," I said. Now, if only I could get everyone to take a wrong turn on another trail, leaving me and Herbert alone, it really would be perfect. "Gee, Mandy, you look awfully relaxed," I commented.

"You're not even pale, like this morning when you looked like death warmed over," Jessica added. "Remember?"

"Yeah. That was awful. But I feel fine now," Mandy said. "Don't worry about me."

It took all my energy not to glare at her. How dare she act sweet and innocent? The more I thought of it, the more I was convinced that Jessica was right: Mandy had some scheme going, and she'd managed to fool us all.

I didn't want Mandy back in the Unicorn Club if she was going to be like that. We'd be much better off without her!

"Cheese and veggie sandwiches OK?" Herbert reached into the saddlebags and pulled out a large square plastic container.

"I thought you had to eat beef at every meal on a dude ranch," Mandy said.

"Maybe in the old days," Herbert replied. "We're a little more flexible now."

"Good. I like cheese better." Lila spread a plaid blanket on the ground and sat down on it. "Ow!"

"Something wrong?" Herbert asked.

"It's kind of hard to sit down," she said. "I think I'm saddle-sore."

"After only a couple of hours?" I scoffed, sitting down beside her and smoothing the blanket. I was desperately hoping that Herbert would sit next to me.

"I didn't realize there was a time requirement," Lila said in a snooty voice. "All I know is that it hurts."

Herbert, Ellen, Mandy, and Jessica came over to join us. Herbert set down all the food in the middle of the blanket and started opening the different containers. "Help yourselves, girls," he said.

I patted the blanket next to me. "Have a seat," I said, trying to sound casual.

He sat down next to me. Victory. I blushed, smiling at him.

Lila squirmed on the blanket. "So what should I do?" she asked in a pitiful voice. "I don't think I can ride all the way back, Herbert."

I watched Lila carefully. Why did I get the sinking feeling that *she* was up to something, too?

Herbert took a sandwich from the container in the middle of the blanket. "Lila, I feel for you, I really do. But there's not really anything you can do. I bet if you walk around a little bit, the pain will go away."

"Maybe it would help if I rode with you on the way back," Lila wheedled.

Immediately, I felt my hands shake with rage. I could have thrown my sandwich at her. "Lila, whether you sit on your saddle or someone else's, it's going to feel exactly the same!" Did she really think that

Herbert couldn't see through her lame suggestion?

"I'm afraid Kimberly's right," Herbert said, shrugging. "One saddle's the same as the next."

Lila turned to me and glared. I thought smoke was actually going to come out of her ears, she looked so mad.

I just grinned at her. "It's hard work, riding all day," I said. "You're just not used to it, I guess."

"You know, I feel a little saddle-sore, too," Jessica announced.

*What are you, stupid?* I wanted to say. That trick hadn't worked for Lila, so why did Jessica think it would work for her? Maybe they'd gotten too much sun, and it had affected their brains.

Jessica stood up. "But I think I'll take your suggestion, Herbert, and wander around a little bit." She picked up a sandwich. "I'll be down at the pond, if anyone wants me."

"OK," I told her. "Have fun." Phew, I thought— at least one person was out of the way. Jessica was probably so mad at Mandy that she didn't even want to sit on the same picnic blanket with her.

"So, Ellen, how are you doing?" Herbert asked, leaning back and crossing his legs. "Are you sore, too?"

Ellen shook her head. "No, I feel fine." She bit into an apple. "I don't know why it's bugging everyone else so much. We've only been riding for a little while."

"You call three and a half hours a little while?" Lila asked.

Ellen shrugged. "Sure. I mean, we've only been

sitting around. The horses are the ones who do all the work."

"How about you, Kimberly?" Herbert asked, turning toward me. "Are you having fun?"

I felt my face flush as our eyes met. "Oh, yeah," I said. "Definitely. Of course—" I broke off.

"What's wrong?" Herbert asked, looking concerned.

"Well, I was wondering if maybe you could show me the more advanced trails sometime," I suggested. "I mean, I know the others aren't exactly at that *level*, but since I've been taking lessons all my *life*—"

Out of the corner of my eye, I could see *both* Lila and Mandy frowning at me. Well, serves them right! If they weren't going to be fair about this, why should I?

"The really tough riding is south of the ranch," Herbert said. "There are plenty of fences to jump over, not to mention lots of tiny streams, and some real muddy parts to look out for. If you came back some weekend, I'd be happy to show you."

I felt a glow of happiness. Herbert wanted me to come to the ranch again, *without* the Unicorns! I imagined myself coming back to ride horses with Herbert next weekend. And the weekend after that, and the weekend after that, and—

"Help!" Suddenly there was a loud, incredibly frightening scream. "You guys—help!"

"That's Jessica," Lila said, jumping to her feet.

"Oh, no, I hope it's not a rattlesnake," Ellen said, as we all got up and ran in the direction of the pond.

"So do I!" I cried.

Herbert was running right beside me, at top speed. "Don't worry—I'll protect you," he said.

I loved the sound of that. It was so romantic, I almost forgot what I was doing.

But when we got closer to the pond, I saw Jessica sprawled out on the ground, face first. My heart started thudding. What if she *had* been bitten by a snake? Would Herbert know how to treat her? Would we have enough time to get her back to the ranch before the poison kicked in?

I practically flew over to her. "Jessica!" I panted. "Jessica, are you OK?"

"What happened?" Lila cried. "Jessica, say something!"

Jessica rolled over onto her side and looked up at us. "I tripped."

"Huh?" I said.

"I caught my heel on that rock and . . . I went flying," Jessica said. "My ankle got totally wrenched. I think I might have broken it."

"You *tripped*?" Lila repeated. "That's it?"

"It hurts!" Jessica said, clutching her foot. "I think it's broken!"

"You'll be OK," I said. "It's probably a sprain. Just relax."

"Kimberly's right. Don't panic, Jessica. I'll take a look at it. Easy now." Herbert crouched down beside her. He gently pulled at her boot, trying to slide it off. "That OK?"

Jessica nodded, her mouth crimped with pain. "Just . . . be careful."

Herbert got her boot off and rested her ankle in his hands. "Does this hurt?"

"Ow!" Jessica cried.

"OK, relax. Here, I'll carry you back to our picnic blanket, and you can have something to drink," Herbert said.

As he picked her up, Jessica threw her arms around his neck. "But, Herbert, how am I ever going to ride back to the ranch?"

I frowned. She sounded like a helpless heroine in an old movie. She practically had a Southern accent. Somehow, her fall seemed a little suspicious. Nobody had *seen* her fall. She'd gone over to the pond all by herself for something, and I had an awful feeling it wasn't to stretch her legs.

I clutched Lila's arm as we walked back to our picnic lunch. "Do you think she's really hurt?" I whispered.

"I don't know, but she seems to have picked up a Southern accent while spraining her ankle," Lila muttered.

"Don't worry," Herbert told Jessica, setting her down carefully on the blanket. I stared at both of them, tapping my toe against the ground. "You can ride with me, and we'll lead your horse."

"What about me?" Mandy asked.

"You can ride with Kimberly," Herbert said.

Oh, great. *Now* I was going to get Mandy? After

she'd hogged Herbert's attention all morning? I didn't want her anywhere near me!

I glared at Jessica, then at Mandy. It was so unfair! *They* got to ride with Herbert, when I was the one who was in love with him!

About fifteen minutes later, we were headed back down the trail, Mandy sitting behind me on Catalina, holding on for dear life, and Jessica perched on Herbert's saddle.

No, not just perched: laughing and singing old country tunes. The pain in her ankle seemed to have completely disappeared. How *odd.*

"Home, home on the range," Jessica warbled. "Where the deer and the an . . . te . . . lope play . . ."

I rolled my eyes. I could think of another verse to that song that was a little more appropriate: Home, home on the range, where my friends are all acting like jerks . . .

Here I was, at one of the nicest dude ranches in the entire country, and I'd never been on a worse ride in my life!

I was the one who really loved Herbert.

And the worst thing was, Jessica *knew* that. And she was throwing herself at him anyway, just as Mandy had.

I was starting to think that I didn't really have any friends at all.

# Eight

"I had a great time, Herbert," Mandy said when we stopped our horses in the corral outside the barn. "Thanks for the ride, Kimberly. I don't even feel afraid of horses anymore."

"I knew we'd make a rider out of you," Herbert said cheerfully.

Mandy giggled nervously. "I just have *one* question, though. How do you get off this thing?" She looked down at the ground uneasily.

"You get off like that," I told Mandy, feeling Herbert's eyes on me. I swung my leg over the saddle and dropped to the ground. "It's very easy." I smiled at Herbert.

"Good job, Kimberly," Herbert told me. Then he turned to Mandy. "I can help you down as soon as I get Jessica," he offered. "She might need to go into town to see the doctor, if this ankle's broken."

"Oh . . . I don't think it's broken," Jessica said. "You know what? It doesn't even hurt anymore."

*Really*, I felt like saying. *You don't say.* "All the same, it's probably a sprain, Jessica—and you know what *that* means," I said. "You won't be able to do any dancing tonight. Too bad. That is *such* a shame."

Jessica's eyes widened with shock. She cleared her throat, as Herbert lifted her off the horse and put her gently down on the ground. She stood on her right foot, lifted her "injured" ankle, and pressed against it with her hand. "Actually, it doesn't hurt at all. It's not even swollen anymore."

"Wow. Talk about a miraculous recovery," Herbert said.

"That's one way of putting it," I muttered.

"It's all because I didn't have to ride on the way back, I guess. It got a chance to heal," Jessica said, looking smugly at me. "Now I'm ready to dance all night!"

Herbert went to help Mandy down, and then he started taking off all the saddles and bridles. When he went into the stables, I stalked over to Jessica. "You are so incredibly juvenile!" I said.

"What do you mean?" Jessica said innocently.

"That phony broken ankle thing!" I cried. "You staged the whole accident just to get Herbert's attention."

"I did not!" Jessica said. "It really hurt."

"Yeah, for about ten seconds," I scoffed. "Until

Herbert came running over and picked you up. Then you played it for all it was worth."

"That was so romantic-looking when he picked you up in his arms," Ellen mused, a dreamy expression on her face. "Like something out of a movie."

"Yeah. A bad, low-budget, spaghetti western B movie, maybe," I sputtered. "Jessica, I can't believe you'd pull a stunt like that. Especially not after we talked last night."

"Talked about what?" Jessica said.

"You know," I said. "I told you how I felt about Herbert!"

Jessica raised her eyebrows. "Gee, I don't remember that."

"Yes, you do," I insisted. "And you know exactly what I'm *referring* to. We talked about it for a long time!"

Jessica looked at me innocently. "Kimberly, I was exhausted last night. I mean, I don't want to insult you or anything, but I think I fell asleep while you were still talking. So I have no idea what you said. Sorry."

I glared at her. "Oh, right. I bet you don't."

"What's the big deal, Kimberly?" Lila asked. "We all like Herbert." She gazed at him in the distance. "I mean, who wouldn't?"

"Yeah, we *all* like him, but *I'm* the one who should be spending time with him," I said. "It was my idea to come here in the first place, and I'm the only serious rider out of all of us."

"Hey, if Herbert likes me better, it's not my fault," Jessica said breezily.

"He doesn't like you!" I said. "He just feels sorry for you, because he *thinks* you hurt yourself."

Jessica stared at me for a second. "Kimberly, you're making a big deal out of nothing. Give it up already." Then she turned to Lila. "Come on, let's go pick out what we're going to wear tonight." The two of them strolled off in the direction of the lodge.

"Look at her!" I fumed, watching Jessica practically jog up the trail. "Why doesn't she just *skip* all the way back? I can't believe her! I can't believe she faked an injury so she could ride with Herbert, when she *knew* how I felt about him."

"Kimberly, don't you think you're getting a little carried away?" Mandy asked, looking timidly at me.

"I'm getting carried away? Oh, that's a good one," I said. "You don't see *me* pretending to break my ankle, do you?"

"No, but—come on, we're here to have fun together. I hate seeing you and Jessica arguing like that over some guy," Mandy said.

"Yeah, it's not worth it," Ellen added. "Remember—we said we wouldn't argue."

I folded my arms. "Yeah, well, I wouldn't, if people weren't acting like total jerks."

Mandy frowned. "Isn't that kind of harsh?" she asked softly.

I groaned. "I'll tell you what's *harsh*. Coming up with a story about being afraid of horses!

You know, you're as bad a traitor as Jessica!"

"It's not a story," Mandy said slowly. "I am afraid. I mean, I was afraid."

"Yeah, you were scared to death the second you figured out that Herbert was our riding instructor and that you could get him to take special care of you," I said angrily. "You're really an inspiration, Mandy. I suppose tonight you'll develop a phobia of line dancing!"

"Kimberly!" Ellen exclaimed. "I don't think that's very nice."

"Maybe you don't believe me, but it's true," Mandy insisted. "It's too bad you can't appreciate how hard it was for me to even get *near* a horse."

"Well, I wish you *hadn't* gotten near a horse," I blurted out. My blood was really boiling now. How dare she stand there and judge me after how she'd lied! "I thought it might be a good idea to have you back in the Unicorns, but I guess I was wrong. Why don't you go call the Angels and see if they'll fly in and take you away?" I stared at Mandy, challenging her to meet my eyes.

She stared back. "Kimberly, I can't even believe you'd say something like that to me." Her lip was quivering, as if she was about to cry.

I crossed my arms over my chest. "Well, can I help it if you're a total liar?"

Mandy kept looking at me for a second, then she shook her head. "At least the Angels know how to be friends." She turned and started running toward the lodge.

"Good riddance," I muttered.

"You didn't have to be so mean to her," Ellen said, looking pained. "Why did you do that?"

"Do what? I was only telling the truth," I declared. "Both she and Jessica are out to ruin my trip here, Ellen. I mean, it's so obvious."

"That's not true!" Ellen cried. "Mandy really is afraid of horses, and Jessica—"

"Don't tell me she really broke her ankle," I cut in.

Ellen looked at me pleadingly. "Why do you have to fight with everyone all the time?" she asked. Then she turned and walked out of the corral.

"But, Ellen, I didn't start this whole thing—"

"I'll talk to you later," Ellen said. "When you're being reasonable again."

"OK, *fine*," I muttered, even though I was the *only* reasonable one, as far as I was concerned.

I went over to Catalina and started stroking her nose. It wasn't my fault, I told myself. I was the one who'd offered everyone a free, fun weekend. And how had they returned the favor? By going after the first guy I liked since I came back to Sweet Valley.

"Friends are overrated," I told Catalina, whose ears flicked at a fly. I knew she was listening. "Be glad you're a horse," I said.

"Hey, there," Herbert said, walking out of the barn a few minutes later. "Feel like lending a hand?" He was carrying a few bristle brushes.

"Definitely!" I said, grinning. The fact that everyone had deserted me and gone back to the lodge had turned out to be *perfect*. Finally, I had Herbert all to myself.

He handed me a brush, his hand lightly grazing mine. I was so surprised, I almost dropped the brush. "Got it?" he asked.

"Oh, uh, yeah," I practically stuttered. "Got it." I smiled at him and followed him over to where the horses were tethered to the corral fence.

"I'm sure I don't have to tell *you* what to do," Herbert said.

"No, I've done this a hundred times," I told him happily, starting to brush Catalina's back.

My heart was racing. I was finally alone with Herbert. This was my big chance. More than anything, I wanted to talk to him. But I just didn't know what to say, or how to start.

"So, um, Herbert," I said. He was brushing the horse next to mine, Summer Sun. Ellen had been riding her. "When we were having lunch, before Jessica's . . . accident. You mentioned something about some harder trails?"

"Oh, yeah. We have several different trails here," he said. "Some are for the guests, and then some are more for the people who work here year-round."

"You mean, like, for you?" I asked.

"Right," Herbert said, running his brush down Summer Sun's side.

"And what are they like?" I moved around Catalina and started brushing her from the other side, so I'd be closer to Herbert and he could see what a fantastic job I was doing.

"They're great trails," Herbert said enthusiastically. "I've been riding here since I was a little kid, you know? And my mother wouldn't even let me go on some of them until a couple of years ago. That's how hard they are."

"You're kidding," I said. "They were too hard even for someone as experienced as you? What are they, impossible?"

Herbert laughed and shook his head. "No, but thanks for the compliment. Actually, the first time I rode one trail, I tried to jump this fallen tree, and wham! My horse reared up and tossed me right into a big pile of mud."

I gasped. "Were you OK?"

Herbert laughed. "Oh, sure—a little dirty, that's all. I had so much mud on me, I looked like the creature from the black lagoon!"

I giggled, picturing Herbert covered in mud, except for his two blue eyes peering out. Two incredibly gorgeous, deep-blue eyes. "What happened after that?" I asked, gazing into his eyes.

"I learned to take things a little more slowly," Herbert said. "The guys here set up a bunch of jumps. Some of them I don't even try. Only an expert rider could make it over them."

*You* are *an expert*, I thought, but I didn't say it.

He seemed like the modest type. "So when do you find the time to ride? I mean, you take guests on guided trips on Saturdays and Sundays."

"I go out riding at night a lot," Herbert explained. "After everyone's asleep and I'm officially off duty."

"Isn't it too dark to see where you're going?" I asked.

"Nah." Herbert finished Summer Sun and moved on to the next horse. "With such big sky out here, as long as the moon's out, I can see just fine. In fact, there's even a trail called the Moonlight Madness Trail."

"Moonlight Madness Trail," I sighed.

Just the sound of those words made me picture Herbert galloping down a trail, leaping over a mountain stream, under a full moon. And I could picture me, right behind him, making all the jumps. We'd stop and catch our breath, looking up at all the stars. Could there *be* anything more romantic?

"You know, you don't have to stick around and help me finish," Herbert said. "You probably want to go wash up before our big barbecue tonight. Get the trail dust off."

Trail dust, I thought, touching my face and wiping off a layer of grit. Ugh! Here I was, hanging around and chatting with Herbert while I looked like a dust ball! Frantically, I began brushing off my face.

Herbert laughed. "Don't worry—you look fine," Herbert said. "As pretty as you did when we left this morning."

I practically fainted. He called me pretty!

Taking the brush from me, Herbert reached out and ruffled my hair with the other. "You're a cute kid, you know that, Kimmie?"

He actually ruffled my hair! He thought I was pretty *and* cute.

So what if nobody had called me "Kimmie" since I was seven?

So what if I usually lost it when anybody called me a kid?

When Herbert said those words, they sounded totally different. They sounded amazing, wonderful . . .

"Well, I'll, uh, see you at dinner, right?" I asked him, my heart pounding.

"You'd better get there early, before I eat all the ribs," Herbert joked.

"OK," I said, smiling. "Hey, thanks for the fun ride today."

"No problem," Herbert responded. "I'll see you tonight! Get ready for some serious line dancing. Maybe we can share the first dance or something."

*The dance!* I thought happily. He was asking me to dance with him—to share the first dance of the whole night! And the first dance would lead to another dance, and another, and pretty soon it would be the last dance and then—

That was when I realized that I'd forgotten to respond. "I'd like that," I said, smiling at him. "I mean, that sounds great."

"OK, see you then!" Herbert called over his shoulder as he headed into the barn.

"Right! See you tonight!" I called back.

I climbed over the fence and started walking up toward the lodge in a daze. There was no doubt about it—Herbert was perfect for me. And it looked as if he knew it, too.

# Nine

"Is *that* what you're going to wear?" Jessica said when I came out of the bathroom after my shower about half an hour later. I was wearing a white blouse with tiny flowers embroidered around the collar, and a short black skirt.

"What's wrong with it?" I said coolly, fastening a silver charm bracelet.

"Nothing," she said with a shrug. "If you want to look younger than your age."

"What do you mean?" I looked at myself in the full-length mirror on the back of the closet door.

"Well, you look like you're about ten, that's all," Jessica said.

I spun around. Jessica was wearing a short red dress that tied in the back and had small black polka dots on it. Instead of cowboy boots, she was wearing her black flats. "Oh, and I suppose you look so much older?" I said. "Haven't you had that dress since at least the fifth grade?"

"Actually, it's brand-new," Jessica said, fastening a silver earring in her left earlobe. "You must have it confused with something else."

*And I must have you confused with someone else,* I added silently. *I thought you were my friend—at least when we left Sweet Valley you were.* Now it was every Unicorn for herself. Well, two could play at that game.

"Jessica, is that my silver barrette you're wearing?" I asked.

"You said I could borrow it yesterday, when we were driving up here," Jessica said, patting the barrette in her hair.

I gave her a blank look. "I don't remember that," I said.

Jessica shrugged. "Well, you did."

"Well, I changed my mind," I argued. "I want to wear it tonight."

Jessica frowned. "As you can see, I'm already wearing it."

"Then take it off!" I cried. "I don't want you to have anything of mine, after the way you've been acting." I folded my arms across my chest and glared at her.

"You know what? I don't even want anything of yours, after the way *you've* been acting!" Jessica unclipped the barrette and tossed it at me. "In fact, I don't even want to share a *room* with you!"

"What took you so long? I've been waiting for you to move out ever since we got here!" I cried.

"Kimberly, you're only jealous because Herbert likes me more than you," Jessica declared, stuffing her clothes into a duffel bag.

"Ha! *That* is the funniest thing I've ever heard!" I exclaimed. "I was just talking to him for practically half an hour, and he promised he'd dance with me first tonight."

"Yeah, right," Jessica scoffed.

"It's true," I replied. "He only felt sorry for you because you pretended to break your dumb ankle. Which is only the most juvenile ploy in the entire world!"

"I'm juvenile? *I'm* juvenile?" Jessica cried. "Look who's talking! You're the one who thinks Herbert likes you, just because he was nice enough to talk to you after you hung around the stables all afternoon, looking pathetic."

"Talk about pathetic!" I shouted. "I'm not the one who lied so Herbert would like me. You seem to be walking just fine now!"

"Oh, yeah? Why don't you watch me walk!" Jessica said. She picked up her bags and stormed out of the room.

"Hi," Ellen said shyly. "I guess we're back to being roommates again." She walked into the bedroom and set her small bag on the floor.

"Good," I said, "you're just in time. Can you

help me with this?" I held up the barrette, which I was having trouble fastening. I was so angry that my hands were shaking.

"Sure," Ellen said. She stood behind me and clipped the barrette around the hair I'd pulled back from the front. "How's that?"

"Great," I said. "Thanks."

"You're welcome," Ellen said with a sigh. She sounded kind of sad.

"What's wrong?" I asked her.

"For one thing, you and Jessica fighting," she said.

"Aren't you guys forgetting the pact we made at lunch yesterday? We all agreed that we'd never let a guy come between us. That in the Unicorns, friends come first, and boys second."

"Yeah, yeah," I said dismissively. "But some things are worth fighting for. At any cost."

"Left behind right, right behind left, turn, scoot, scoot, step-slide, step-slide—"

"Hold on, I'm getting dizzy," I told Mrs. Margot. I knew that getting Mandy to teach me some line dancing was out of the question, so I went to Mrs. Margot for help. The only trouble was, she knew so many moves that I was getting confused.

"Watch me again," Mrs. Margot said patiently. She moved across the kitchen floor, turning, stepping, scooting, stomping her heels against the floor, turning back toward me. "Now do you get it?"

I laughed. "Not exactly. Where's the part when

you tap your left heel with your right hand, and vice versa?" That was the part I recognized from TV.

"That's a different dance. Here—you stand behind me, and just copy the moves I call out," Mrs. Margot said. "As I say them, we'll both do them. You'll be doing fine in a jiffy."

I felt a tingle of excitement as she showed me the moves again. Even if I didn't become a line-dancing star in a matter of minutes, I was still going to dance with Herbert. That was what really mattered.

"Y'all can help yourselves to everything else on the buffet table, all right?" Terry, one of the Sunset Dude Ranch cooks, put a huge plate of burgers on our picnic table out on the front lawn.

"All right!" Jessica said, leaning forward on the bench. "This food looks awesome."

"Let's try to get through dinner without anyone fighting, OK?" Ellen said, looking sternly at all of us. Ellen and I were sitting on one side of the picnic table, and Mandy, Lila, and Jessica were on the other. "It really kills my appetite."

"Who wants to argue?" Lila said. "I want to *eat!*"

So did I. There were burgers and ribs cooking on the grill, and there was a long buffet table behind us covered with bowls of different salads, cans of soda, and bottles of extra-hot and extra-sweet barbecue sauce. My mouth was watering, I was so hungry.

But if Ellen thought I was just going to forget about what traitors the other Unicorns were, she was crazy.

Lila grabbed a burger and put it on her plate. "I'm starting with this for an appetizer."

"Me too. I love barbecued food," Mandy said. She took a huge bite of a burger. "Especially hamburgers. This one's great."

"Actually, they're buffalo burgers," I told her casually.

Mandy put her bun down. "Buffalo?" She looked as though she was about to be sick.

I nodded. "Mrs. Margot told me earlier, in the kitchen."

"What were you doing in the kitchen?" Lila asked.

"Oh, nothing. Mrs. Margot was just teaching me some dance steps." *So there,* I felt like saying. "I learned all about line dancing—the Achy Breaky, the Boot Scootin' Boogie, the Six Shooter—"

"Wait a second," Jessica said. "Let me get this straight. You've been practicing dancing all afternoon?"

I shrugged. "Only the past half hour or so. But I learned a lot. Mrs. Margot gave me a real crash course."

"Why didn't you tell us?" Lila asked. "I could use a lesson, too."

Jessica narrowed her eyes. "She didn't *tell* us because she wants to look better than the rest of us tonight."

"Jessica, remember what you said to me the other night," I said calmly.

"What was that? Turn out the light?" she said sarcastically.

I shook my head. "Does the phrase 'All's fair in love and war' sound familiar?"

"A little *too* familiar," Ellen grumbled.

"If you think that Herbert's going to dance with you all night, you'd better get over it, fast," Jessica said.

"Why? Do you actually think he'll dance with someone who has a sprained ankle?" I replied.

"Sooner than he'd dance with somebody who's mean to her friends," Mandy retorted.

"OK, you guys, stop it!" Ellen cried. "We're supposed to be having fun. The dancing hasn't even started yet, so just cut it out."

Lila rolled her eyes. "Whatever you say, Officer Riteman."

"Yeah, who died and made you hall monitor?" Jessica demanded.

"You guys could at least be nice to Ellen," Mandy said. "It's not like *she* did anything." She glanced across the table at me.

"Yeah," I agreed, "it's not like she pretended to be afraid of horses. What's next, Mandy—are you afraid of buffalo burgers?" I pointed to the uneaten burger on her plate.

Mandy glared at me. "The concept's just kind of *strange*, OK?"

"I guess the *Angels* don't rough it very well," I said, snapping open a napkin and putting it in my lap.

"They sure wouldn't act this way," Mandy muttered. "Have you guys forgotten that I was a Unicorn once, too?"

"No, but *you* seem to have," I said.

"What's that supposed to mean?" Mandy asked.

"Unicorns don't go around stabbing each other in the back," I replied. "Except, of course, for Jessica over here."

"Does anyone want some potato salad?" Ellen said nervously, standing up from the table.

"I think I'll go with you," Lila said. "You guys are completely interfering with my digestion. I *might* bring you some iced tea or something, if you'd stop arguing long enough to say please."

"I only pretended to get hurt after *she* pretended to be scared," Jessica said, ignoring Lila. "It's all Mandy's fault, so don't try to blame anything on me, Kimberly."

"But I didn't make anything up," Mandy protested, tears welling up in her eyes.

"Oh, give it up," I told her. "We're not falling for that story again." I stood up and tossed my napkin onto the table. "I think I'll see if I can sit somewhere else."

"And how are you all doing tonight? Hey, Kimmie."

I spun around, practically knocking Herbert

over. "H-hi," I stammered. I hadn't even heard him come up.

"Hi, Herbert!" Jessica said enthusiastically.

Mandy sniffled, wiping the tears off her face.

"Oh, no! Mandy, what's wrong?" Herbert rushed to her side.

She shook her head. "N-nothing."

"Oh, now, come on—we're good friends, aren't we? Tell me what's got you so upset," Herbert said.

*Good friends?* Because she'd forced him to take care of her all afternoon?

"No, I'm OK," Mandy said. "Really. Thanks, though." She sniffled, and dabbed at her eyes again.

"Gosh. I just hate to see you having a bad time," Herbert said.

"She'll get over it," Jessica told him, smiling. "I mean, I'll help her as much as I can. Of course. Mandy, isn't there *anything* I can do?" she said in a sickly-sweet voice.

I just stood there, unable to move or speak, while Herbert wrapped his arm around Mandy's shoulders and squeezed her. It was like an instant replay of that morning, when he helped her onto her horse.

"Cheer up, Mandy," Herbert said. "You've got great friends, no matter what happens, right? You told me you guys are all in one tight club, the Unicorns, right—best friends?"

"Actually, Mandy's not officially a Unicorn," I told Herbert. And she wasn't going to be, anytime soon.

"Maybe not, but we'll always be there for you, Mandy, no matter what stunt you pull," Jessica said. "Ahem, I mean, no matter what happens."

Mandy looked down at the table, still crying.

"I've got an idea," Herbert said, handing Mandy a napkin. "So that your dude ranch vacation isn't a total washout, Mandy, I am personally going to teach you how to line-dance tonight. In fact, I'm going to dance with you to the very first song. How does that sound?"

As Mandy looked up at him, her eyes glistening with tears, my heart sank to the ground.

*That sounds wrong—very wrong!* "But, Herbert— you and I—you promised *me* the first dance," I sputtered.

Herbert stood up and came closer to me. "I know, Kimmie, but Mandy needs me. Can't you see she's upset?"

"Oh, I can see, all right," I muttered angrily. *And don't call me Kimmie,* I felt like yelling.

"You understand, don't you?" Herbert asked sweetly.

*Yes, I understand,* I thought, glaring at Mandy, who looked up at me. She'd stopped crying, but I felt as though I was about to start. How could I ever have thought of Mandy as my friend?

# Ten

"Come on, Kimberly. You can't stand here all night," Ellen said. "Don't you want to dance?"

I tapped my boot against the large wooden deck outside the lodge, where the band was playing. "Not exactly," I said, watching the line of people in front of me all making the same dance moves.

"You mean, you don't want to dance with me," Ellen said. "OK, I'm a little offended, but I'll get over it." She poked my arm. "Ha ha. That was a joke. Get it?"

I turned to her and frowned. "I got it. What I also got is that Jessica's been dancing for the past half hour, and she keeps moving over to where Herbert is."

"Maybe it's just . . . a coincidence," Ellen said. "You know, there are a lot of people out there.

Everyone except us, really. It's not like they're the only ones on the dance floor."

I stared at Herbert as Jessica spun around and bumped into him. He laughed, then turned her around to face the right way. She was laughing, too. Then Mandy did the same thing, with Lila right behind her.

Once again, everyone was having a great time—except me. Once again, Jessica was claiming all of Herbert's attention—that is, after Mandy had danced next to him for the first two songs. Why was I even surprised anymore?

"Come on, Kimberly, let's just get out there," Ellen said. "Once we start dancing, Herbert's bound to come join us."

"I don't know." I watched as Herbert smoothly tapped his hands against his boot heels. He was good at *every*thing.

"Do you want to show him you can dance or not?" Ellen demanded. "I thought you were good."

"Well, all right," I said, giving in. It was worth *one* last shot, anyway. "Let's go."

The band had just started playing a new song, and Mrs. Margot stepped up to the microphone. "And now, won't you all join me in the Boot Scootin' Boogie!"

"Hey, this is one I know," I said, perking up a little.

Ellen looked at me and shrugged. "I can give it a shot, I guess."

There were three lines of dancers on the floor.

We stepped into the middle of one, right behind Lila, Mandy, Jessica, and Herbert. I decided to watch only Herbert.

He was so cute, stomping and clapping his way around, that it was hard for me to keep track of my *own* feet.

I put my right heel out, then crossed it back, turned my left foot out, and back. Then I scooted forward on my right foot, stepped to the left, and kicked and clapped. I kicked so high, my boot almost hit Jessica in the rear end! *Now that would be some good line dancing,* I thought with a smile, as we all moved to the right, crossed our feet behind, and kicked and clapped again. This time I almost hit Mandy.

Herbert glanced over his shoulder at me and gave me the thumbs-up signal.

"Did you see that?" I gasped to Ellen.

She nodded. "I told you all we had to do was get out here. Isn't this fun?" she called to me above the noise.

"I love it!" I said. Spinning around, I saw Herbert take a step backward, coming toward me and Ellen. He did it so smoothly, as if it were part of the dance.

Was he coming to dance with me? Yes, that had to be it—only he was being really sly and casual about it, so nobody's feelings would get hurt. I stepped toward him, sidling closer. I moved to the right . . .

He moved to the left. He stepped around me

and went over to dance beside Ellen. "How's it going, El? Nice moves! Done this before?"

"No, it's the first time!" she said, grinning.

*El?* What, did he have a nickname for everybody?

I moved back toward him, determined to get his attention. "Hi, Herbert!"

But he didn't even hear me. He'd already started moving through the crowd, dancing with those stupid little twins, Justin and Jake!

It wasn't fair! Jessica and Mandy had already had *their* dances with Herbert, and now he was off mingling with the guests. It was probably something he had to do, but still. He didn't have any time left for me, the girl he'd promised the first dance to.

I took one last kick in the general direction of Jessica and Mandy and walked off the dance floor.

"Hi, Kimberly," Lila said. "How's it going?"

I turned around from the snack table and shrugged. *How do you think?* I felt like saying. Mandy and Jessica walked off the dance floor toward us, and I turned back around. I didn't have one thing to say to either one of them, except maybe "Get lost!"

"Don't you just *love* this whole scene?" Mandy said. "It's a full moon, we're up in the mountains, dancing the night away . . . I don't think anyone's going to believe us back home when we tell them how beautiful it was."

"I *know*," Jessica gushed.

Yeah, and nobody back home would believe me when I told them how horrible it was, either, I thought.

"Hey, do you guys want anything?" Jessica asked. "Cookies, crackers, punch?"

"Since when do you wait on anybody?" Lila said, teasing her.

"The mountain air must have affected her brain," Mandy joked.

Jessica looked offended. "Just for that, I'll get each of you a cup of punch, whether you want one or not. Even Kimberly."

"What's that supposed to mean?" I grumbled.

"Oh, nothing," Jessica said innocently, smiling at me. She turned to the punch bowl and started filling five huge cups with the red, fruity-looking drink.

I glared at her back. Sure, she could be in a good mood and want to make up. She'd been having a good time. I, on the other hand, had never been more miserable. On top of having the line dance ruined, I'd been so upset during dinner that I hadn't eaten a thing. I was about to grab a chocolate chip cookie off the table when I saw Herbert making his way through the crowd toward me.

*Finally!* I thought.

"Hey, Kimmie, how's it going?" he said cheerfully.

"It's going great," I said. *Now it is, anyway!* "Want a cookie?" I handed one to him, and he crunched into it.

"Thanks. Hey, I've barely seen you all night," Herbert said. "I can't believe it's the last dance already!"

"Neither can I," I said. I *really* couldn't believe it. My dream was coming true. Who really cared about the first dance? He'd been saving the *last* dance for me, and that was much more important. This way it would only be natural for us to hang out a little bit afterward, talking or walking or just gazing at the gorgeous full moon.

"Now, I *know* you can do a mean Waltz Across Texas," Herbert said.

I couldn't help giggling. I'd never even heard of a waltz like that. "I can?"

"Sure," Herbert said. "It's easy. I'll help you."

He reached out for my hand, and I turned toward him. At the same moment, Jessica turned around from the table and held out a large, full plastic cup. "Here's your punch, Kimberly!"

Her hand bashed into my arm, and the cup went flying, splashing bright-red punch all over my white shirt. "Jessica!" I cried. "Look what you did!"

"Oh, my gosh," she gasped. "I'm so sorry, Kimberly."

"You're *sorry*?" I said.

"What can I do? I feel awful!" She grabbed a napkin off the table and started rubbing my blouse with it—only the napkin had barbecue sauce on it and made things even worse.

"You feel awful!" I exclaimed, staring down at

my disgustingly dirty blouse. "You—you did this on purpose!"

"What?" Jessica sounded shocked. "It was a complete accident!"

"Girls, it's OK," Herbert began. "I can—"

"It's not OK!" I yelled. "Nothing's OK!" I was standing there, in front of the boy I wanted to dance with more than anything in the world—he'd even asked me to dance—and now I couldn't because Jessica had spilled punch on me and rubbed barbecue sauce on my shirt on top of that!

Jessica was shaking her head. "Kimberly, I didn't mean to—"

"Listen," Mandy said to me, "I'll go upstairs with you. You can change your shirt and be back in time for the last dance."

I rolled my eyes. Did they really think I was *that* naive? I'd seen their innocent act before—I didn't believe it then, and I definitely didn't believe it now. They'd planned the whole thing!

I turned and ran to our suite as fast as I could, taking the steps two at a time. There was a lock on the door between our two rooms, but we hadn't used it yet.

I went into my room and bolted the door behind me. Then I collapsed on my bed, punch-stained blouse and all, and burst out crying. Everything was going wrong!

After what had just happened, I could forget about Herbert becoming my boyfriend. And I could forget about being a Unicorn! I didn't want to belong to a club that would even consider having Mandy and Jessica as members!

"I can't believe the band did two encores!"

"And I can't believe Herbert dipped you halfway to the floor during that Texas Two-Step."

"He's the best, isn't he?"

I opened one eye and glared at the closed door. Did they have to talk so loud? Couldn't they tell a person was trying to sleep in the other room?

OK, maybe I wasn't really trying to sleep. Actually, I was lying there, going over and over the horrible evening in my head. It was all Jessica's fault that I hadn't been able to enjoy the encores, or dance that Texas waltz with Herbert. I'd never forgive her for that, I told myself—never. I punched my pillow and turned over.

"Too bad Herbert can't come back to Sweet Valley with us," I heard Jessica saying.

"Yeah, he'd be a major addition to the social life. Major," Lila added.

"I don't think he'd like it there very much," Mandy mused. "He's into the wide-open-spaces concept."

*So am I,* I thought. *And right now, I wish there were a wide open space between me and everyone in that room.*

"Kimberly's probably been sleeping this whole time," Ellen said. "It's too bad she had to leave right when he asked her to dance."

"Yeah, it is too bad," Mandy agreed. "I felt awful."

Yeah, right. I'm sure she felt awful—for at least half a second. I knew Mandy was just trying to look nice in front of Ellen, the only one who actually seemed to care about my feelings.

"I felt awful, too," Jessica said. "But then Herbert danced with me and it all kind of flew out of my mind. I just love the Waltz Across Texas." She sighed loudly. "I'm never going to forget tonight."

*Neither am I!* I thought, fuming. So it was true— she'd deliberately spilled punch on me so *she* could have the last dance with Herbert. He'd probably told her he was going to ask me to dance with him, and she made sure that would never happen. And on top of that, she'd gotten to dance with him during all the encores, while I was in the bathroom soaking my stupid shirt!

"Well, I'm pretty tired. I think I'll go to bed," Ellen said. "Good night, you guys." I heard her fiddling with the doorknob between the two rooms.

I reached over and twisted the lock on the door, so she could get in.

"Kimberly?" she said tentatively, as she stepped into the room. "Are you awake?"

"I am now," I grumbled.

"Sorry," she said, stepping quietly over to the dresser.

I just lay there with the covers over my head. I was so mad I was practically shaking, but I didn't want to take it out on Ellen. She didn't deserve it.

Besides, I knew that getting angry wouldn't solve anything. What I needed was a plan.

I pulled the covers down and stared out the window beside my bed for a minute. The light from the full moon was streaming through the window.

That's when I remembered the Moonlight Madness Trail. It was a perfect night for a ride. And if I thought so, Herbert was bound to think the same thing.

I could meet him out there, impress him with my jumping skills, show him what a terrific rider I was . . . And then he would see that *I* was the only girl for him. After our ride, we'd come back to the corral and sit on the fence together under the full moon. . . .

Suddenly, I could care less about dancing the Texas waltz. I knew exactly what I had to do.

# Eleven

"Walk on, Catalina. Easy now." I had already saddled Catalina, by the light of a bare bulb left on in the stable. Now I was leading her out of her stall, toward the door. "This is going to be fun," I told her. On our way out the door, I grabbed a helmet off the row of them hanging on hooks on the wall.

It was very creepy being outdoors by myself. About a million crickets were chirping. An owl hooted. I shivered as I put my foot in the stirrup and climbed onto Catalina. I'd forgotten how much the temperature went down in the mountains at night.

I led Catalina out of the corral and through the field, down toward the south side of the ranch. All I had to do was find the Moonlight Madness Trail. I was sure Herbert would be out riding. In the open field, I could see everything, thanks to the full moon.

Catalina walked confidently, as if she knew where she was going, her hooves clopping against the rocky trail. After a few minutes, I came to a crossing: one trail went left, one trail to the right. I chewed my thumbnail. Which one would lead me to Herbert? Catalina seemed to be pulling me toward the one on the right. "What is it, girl?" I said.

She stepped closer to the trail. My eyes lit on a small sign carved out of wood. It had a quarter-moon on it, and the initials "M.M.T."

"All right! Good job," I told Catalina, petting her mane. Then I squeezed her with my legs, and she took off at a gentle trot. *Go slow,* a little voice inside me said. *You don't know the trail.*

But I didn't *feel* like going slow. Nothing had gone my way all day—I was going to do this ride the way *I* wanted. I urged Catalina on, and she moved from a quick trot to a canter, striding around a corner and coming up on a narrow creek. I pressed her forward, and she jumped over the creek bed with ease.

I pushed her into a gallop. We headed straight for the next jump, a low-lying white fence, which was kind of broken down. I remembered all the things I'd learned: how to lean forward in the saddle, how to keep my hands light on the reins. I slowed her to a controlled canter as we approached the jump.

"Come on, Catalina," I whispered. She lowered her head, tucked up her forelegs, and sailed into the air. We landed cleanly on the other side. I glanced backward for a second, wondering if Herbert was following me, whether he'd just seen my amazing jump. I didn't see anything but the white fence glowing in the moonlight.

I turned back around as we headed into a darker, woodsy area. Tall trees kept the moonlight from shining through. I slowed Catalina down just a little, and made my way along the rocky trail. I could hear all the night sounds: frogs, owls, crickets. If only Herbert would come up right now, I thought, gazing at a large boulder. This was the perfect, secluded, romantic spot for us to sit, and talk, and maybe kiss. . . .

Suddenly, I heard a rustling in the trees. At first I thought it was just the wind. Then it sounded like something moving toward me. "H-hello?" I said softly, pulling up on the reins.

I heard only more rustling in reply. *OK, Kimberly, don't freak out,* I told myself. *It's probably just a mouse. Or a rabbit. Or . . . a dog. Or . . . an extremely large, menacing grizzly bear with huge teeth.*

*Oh, no,* I thought. *Or a rattlesnake.* If it was a rattlesnake, Catalina would freak out, and dump me onto the ground next to it!

But Catalina didn't seem the slightest bit afraid. I took a few deep breaths. Whatever was making that noise, she was used to it. Which might mean . . .

Could it be? Was it possible? Was it a person? Was it Herbert?

He was out here, waiting for me! He'd told me about the Moonlight Madness Trail that afternoon when we were alone. He was hinting for me to meet him here!

"Herbert?" I called into the dark. "Herbert, it's me, Kimberly!"

A large owl suddenly flew right at me, its round eyes glowing in the dark. I ducked as it started swooping down toward my head. "Ahhhhhh!" I cried, scared half to death.

I squeezed Catalina, pressing her to run as fast as she could. My heart was pounding. She galloped down the trail at top speed. I glanced backward to see if the owl was coming after us. Nothing.

Then I turned back around. There was a huge redwood log jump lying across the trail—two feet in front of us! "Wait—Catalina—"

I hesitated, and Catalina balked. She reared up on her hind legs, and I went crashing onto the hard dirt trail, flat on my back. My head whacked against the ground, and I landed with my left leg underneath me, my ankle twisted all the way around.

"Ow," I moaned, wincing as I sat up and straightened my leg. I tried to stand up, but when I put weight on my ankle, it collapsed, and I fell to the ground again. "Catalina?" I called out. "Catalina!" I crawled onto my knees and peered into the darkness.

That's when I saw Catalina's tail disappearing back down the trail, in the direction from where we'd come. She was running at top speed.

"No," I moaned. "This is not happening to me— it *can't* be!"

I was stranded. My ankle was throbbing. Catalina was gone. And needless to say, Herbert wasn't anywhere in sight.

I couldn't make it back to the lodge unless I crawled on my hands and knees. I was going to have to lie out here all night. All by myself. Without anyone else in sight. Surrounded by owls and snakes.

I looked nervously at the ground around me. A tear streaked down my cheek. I shivered and wrapped my arms around myself.

My friends wouldn't even notice I was gone until morning.

I pictured them waking up and wondering where I was. Then my stomach knotted. Would they even care?

Probably not, I thought with a shiver, remembering how horribly we'd been treating one another this whole weekend. Suddenly, every mean thing I'd said and done the day before came back to me. Even if my friends weren't always playing fair, I *was* acting like a jerk. I was so desperate for Herbert to be my boyfriend, I didn't care how I treated my friends. I'd done just what we'd pledged not to do: choose a guy over a friend. Not just one friend—four of them.

And look where it had gotten me. I was all alone in the dark, scary night.

I must have been lying there for about fifteen minutes when I heard horse hooves in the distance. I sat up and looked around. It sounded as though they were coming from the direction of the barn.

"Catalina?" I whispered. Then I realized it was more than one horse. And whoever it was, they were coming right toward me!

*Now* what was I going to do? I looked around for a bush or a tree I could crawl over to and hide behind. There was a pine tree not too far away, and I started crawling toward it, wincing each time I used my ankle.

"Kimberly!"

I collapsed onto the ground with relief, pine needles prickling my hands. That was Jessica's voice! "Jessica!" I called back. "Over here!"

As the two horses came out of the wooded area, I made out two faces: Jessica was riding bareback, and behind her was . . . Mandy? Riding Catalina? Was this a dream?

"Kimberly, what happened?" Mandy asked as she got closer. She and Jessica stopped beside me.

"And why are you on the ground?" Jessica looked down doubtfully.

"I tried to jump that log," I explained tearfully. "I fell off Catalina and— Wait a second, Mandy. What are you doing on Catalina, anyway? I thought you were really afraid of riding."

"She was terrified, but she tried to forget about it because we had to find you," Jessica said softly.

I looked from Jessica to Mandy. "You did? Why? I mean, how did you know where I was and everything?" *And why did you even bother,* I almost added. In a weird way, I couldn't help feeling as if I didn't even deserve to be rescued. Lying on the ground all night would have given me a lot of time to think about things.

"I went to talk to you, after everyone went to sleep," Mandy said. "I was feeling really awful about . . . well, about everything."

"Everything?" I repeated.

Mandy toyed with the end of the reins. "Well, us not getting along, for one. And how the night ended for you, and how you thought I planned something against you. I just couldn't fall asleep—I had to talk to you. But when I went into your room, you were gone."

"Mandy woke me up, because she was worried," Jessica explained. "We waited a little while, to see if you'd come back, but you didn't. We figured you probably went down to the stables, because Mandy had heard you and Herbert talking about the trails during lunch."

"Yeah. I thought I was going to meet him out here," I admitted. "If you can believe anything that dumb."

"Did you guys make a plan?" Jessica sounded surprised.

"No—never mind," I said, shaking my head. The whole thing was too humiliating to even confess to her. "So, um, how did you end up on Catalina?" I asked Mandy nervously.

"Just as we got to the barn, Catalina came running into the corral, looking all frantic." Mandy stroked the horse's neck.

"So *I* told Mandy, if Catalina had left you, it probably meant you were in trouble. 'Cause horses do that, right? Or is that Lassie . . . ?" Jessica mused. "Anyway, I knew we'd need more than one horse to get you back, so I convinced Mandy to get on."

"It's hard to hold on to the reins when your hands are shaking, you know?" Mandy joked. "So was Catalina right? *Are* you hurt?"

I nodded. "I think I sprained my ankle." I tried to stand up, and my leg crumpled beneath me. "Ow!" I cried as my knee landed on a rock.

"Oh, no!" Jessica slid off her horse and dropped to the ground beside me. "Here, I'll help you." She reached out and pulled me to my feet, then supported my weight by putting my arm around her shoulder. "OK, we're going to put you on Catalina, with Mandy."

"Wait a second," I said. "I mean—thanks, but . . . wait. I want to say something first."

Mandy sighed. "I know. You probably don't want to ride with me, after everything that happened," she said in a rush. "But Kimberly, I wasn't pretending to be afraid just so Herbert would ride with me. And to-night? When I started crying? I was really upset. I was so glad when you asked me to come this weekend, and I was trying really hard, but—I don't know. After we met Herbert, everything started going wrong."

"You don't have to tell me," I said, hanging my head. "After we met Herbert was when all our problems started. And I know it's partly my fault."

"And mine," Jessica admitted, helping me over to Catalina. "I know you really liked Herbert, Kimberly.

But I couldn't help myself—I liked him, too!"

"We *all* did," Mandy said. "More or less."

"Yeah, and we made the mistake of acting just like Janet did," Jessica said. "I went out of my way to get him to like me. As if I don't have better things to do with my weekend!"

I shook my head. "I was just as bad as you, Jessica. And . . . well, I just feel terrible, and I'm sorry," I blurted. "To both you guys—and Ellen and Lila. And I think I might have even offended Mrs. Margot in there somewhere, too."

Jessica stared at me for a moment. "Wait a second." Her eyes grew wide. "Don't tell me Kimberly Haver is actually *apologizing* for something."

"Catalina, are you getting this?" Mandy said, rubbing the back of the horse's ears.

I felt myself blush in the darkness. "Well, don't get *used* to it or anything," I said, trying not to smile. "It might not happen again." I sighed. "I mean, I didn't make up any stories, but I was so obsessed over Herbert that I totally lost track of what good friends you guys are. I'm sorry I acted like such a jerk today."

"Well, that makes two of us," Jessica said, smiling sheepishly.

Mandy cleared her throat. "I believe we'll be needing a table for three?"

I looked at her. "You didn't do anything. You really were afraid and everything—you weren't just pretending."

"Well, *no*, but—well, I'm not *completely* innocent either." Mandy looked embarrassed. "When Herbert asked me to dance, and you said he'd already asked you? I should have told him to dance with you. Only I was so mad at you by then that I kind of enjoyed it, which is really dumb."

I smiled at her. "Well, join the club."

Jessica adjusted my arm around her shoulder. "I have an idea. Next time let's not go to a dude ranch. Let's go to, like, a beach in Hawaii."

"OK, but you're paying," I said. "And it has to be a secluded beach. No boys walking by for us to get all stupid about."

"How could we get so wrapped up over someone named Herbert, anyway?" Mandy asked, shaking her head.

"He wasn't even *that* good a singer," Jessica said.

I looked at her. "Yes he was," I said.

"As if we even like country-western music!" Jessica said.

"Actually, I do," Mandy said.

"Well, then he's not the best horse rider trail guide riding instructor person or whatever in the entire world!" Jessica declared. "Is he?" she asked me tentatively.

We all started laughing. "Definitely not," I said.

"Come on. Let's get back to the lodge and tell everyone Kimberly's OK," Jessica said. She helped me climb onto Catalina, in front of Mandy, who helped pull me up into the saddle.

"Thanks," I told her. "Want to take the reins?" I held them back toward her.

She shook her head. "Once was enough. But thanks for offering."

"That's incredible," Ellen said once I had finished explaining what had happened. "What kind of owl was it?"

Lila giggled and rolled her eyes. "The point is, Kimberly's OK." She looked at me. "We were really worried."

"I would have been fine if I hadn't gotten distracted," I said. "I was having a really good time, doing some harder riding, jumping . . ."

"Next time, just do it in the daylight," Lila said. "Then you won't get scared by owls."

I nodded. "Good advice." I was sitting on Lila's bed with an ice-cube-filled towel wrapped around my ankle that Ellen had crept down to the kitchen to prepare. Mandy had propped pillows behind me, so I was comfortable.

It was after two o'clock. I was completely exhausted. I yawned, covering my mouth with my hand.

"Maybe we should all go to bed now," Ellen said. "Mrs. Margot's going to be ringing that huge bell in a couple of hours."

I nodded. "OK. But there's something I want to say first."

"Kimberly, I think you said it all before," Mandy told me.

I shook my head. "Not everything. Look, you guys. I'm sorry I've been acting like such a jerk. I don't even deserve for you to be so nice to me like this, after how I've been. I guess . . . I don't know. I forgot that my friends are way more important than any guy."

"I knew we ought to make that pledge at lunch yesterday more serious," Lila said.

Jessica shrugged. "What did you want us to do, draw blood? I mean, part of being a Unicorn is learning things—"

"The hard way," Mandy interrupted.

"Exactly." Jessica grinned sheepishly. "But I'm sorry, too. I wasn't acting very nice myself. And I definitely wasn't acting like a Unicorn! Next time we meet a guy we all like, let's remind ourselves that friends come first, OK?"

"Deal," I said, shaking her hand. "Is that OK with everybody?"

Mandy nodded. "For sure."

"And do you think you can forgive me for being such a creep to you today?" I asked nervously.

Mandy nodded. "I already have."

"OK. Then I only have one more really important thing to ask you, Mandy."

"What is it?" she asked.

I took a deep breath. "*Now* are you ready to re-join the Unicorns?"

# Twelve

Mandy rearranged practically everything on top of the dresser. Finally, she turned to me. "I'm sorry, Kimberly. But I just can't decide!" She sounded positively miserable. "I love being friends with you guys, but I love being an Angel, too!"

"Well, you can't belong to both clubs," I said firmly. "It won't work."

"It won't, will it?" Mandy said sadly.

"Won't it?" Ellen asked. "I mean, couldn't it?"

"How?" Jessica argued. "She wouldn't even have time to, like, wash her hair."

"Look at it this way," I urged Mandy. "You like being in both clubs, OK. But the Unicorns need you more than the Angels do. I mean, we rely on you. I'd still be lying on that stupid trail if it weren't for you. And Jessica, too, of course." I smiled at

Jessica, glad we weren't fighting anymore.

"And there are tons of other things we need you for," Jessica added.

"Like fashion advice," Ellen chimed in. "For instance, these pajamas I'm wearing are extremely lame." She frowned at the pink plaid flannel shorts and top.

Mandy laughed. "Not to mention your slippers."

"Seriously, Mandy. What do you think?" I pressed. I wanted an answer—and I wanted the answer to be "Unicorns."

Mandy looked at all of us thoughtfully. "You guys have been great to me," she began. "We always have tons of fun, but on top of that, you were really there for me when I was sick and in the hospital. I never would have made it through that without you." She seemed to be on the verge of tears.

"So what's the problem?" I said, trying to keep things light. I couldn't take more than one or two major emotional scenes per day.

"I don't know," she said, putting her hand to her forehead. "It's just that I like what the Angels are trying to do as a club. I want to help other people, I really do. It makes me feel good, and it reminds me that even though I had cancer, other people have problems, too."

While she was talking, I thought about the different good deeds the Angels had done. The fund-raising things. The day-care center. I remembered the car wash the Angels were planning for the following weekend. Mandy had asked us to help, and I'd turned her down without even considering the idea. Would it be awful to team up with the Angels—just this once? If it would help Mandy choose us as her club over the Angels, it'd be worth sacrificing our Saturday.

I sat up a little straighter on the bed. "Mandy, maybe you can't decide tonight, and I guess that's OK. But I've been thinking. Maybe the Unicorns should help out at that car wash next Saturday, after all. Working as a team, we'll probably raise twice as much money."

Mandy's eyes lit up. "That's a great idea!" She came over and hugged me.

"Yeah, great," Lila muttered. "If you like wearing those blue coverall things with your name stitched on the pocket."

I laughed. Even if Mandy didn't rejoin the Unicorn Club right away, she was bound to, eventually. After all, nobody could resist the best club in school forever.

"So what happens today?" Ellen asked, sleepily rubbing her eyelids. We had all risen at the clanging of the bell and dressed quickly for breakfast. "Is there a reason we're up so early?"

"Besides seeing Herbert again . . ." Jessica said.

*"What?"* I asked, staring at her.

She laughed. "No, I was just kidding. We have that huge rodeo exhibition to go to, remember?"

"We don't have to ride, right?" Mandy said.

"No, we just sit there and watch other people do that," I told her.

"Phew." She pretended to wipe sweat from her brow.

"Good," Lila agreed. "I was just starting to be able to sit down again without wincing in pain."

"You're a delicate flower, Lila," Mandy said, her eyes twinkling.

I giggled. "And *I'm* starving. Let's get downstairs." I hopped over to the door, trying not to put any weight on my bad ankle. Ellen took my arm as we went down the stairs. When we walked into the dining room, I almost fell over, even though I was holding on to Ellen's arm.

Standing right inside the front screen doors was Herbert, looking as handsome as usual. Only I could barely see his face, because he was busy kissing a tall redheaded girl! He must have heard us coming down the stairs, because he gave her one last quick kiss, then turned around.

"Hey, here comes my favorite group!" Herbert said, grinning at all of us.

*There goes my heart*, I thought, staring at the way his arms were wrapped around her waist. He pulled himself away long enough to smile at me.

"Unicorn Club of Sweet Valley, I'd like you to meet Gladys O'Reilly, my girlfriend," Herbert said cheerfully.

"Hi . . . Gladys," Mandy said slowly, one of her eyebrows shooting up.

"What are you doing here?" Jessica practically

demanded. "Do you live around here or what?"

She shook her head, her green eyes shining. "No, I live in the city, but I miss Herbert so much when he goes away for these weekends that I decided to surprise him with a visit. And boy, am I glad I did." She looked at him and smiled, and he put his arm around her shoulders.

"Is that an awesome girlfriend, or what?" Herbert said.

"Yeah. Awesome," I said, my face heating up. I couldn't believe I'd been riding like mad the night before, looking for Herbert—when all along, he was probably fast asleep in his bunk, dreaming about Gladys!

"Kimmie, what happened to your ankle?" Herbert stared at the Ace bandage wrapped around it. (Ellen's mother had made her pack a first-aid kit.)

"Oh, it's nothing," I told him. "Just a little sprain."

"Well, when did you do that?" Herbert asked.

I shot everyone a panicked look. I wasn't about to announce I was out looking for him in the moonlight!

"She . . . fell," Mandy said.

"On one of my . . . shoes," Jessica added. "I'm an incredibly messy roommate. I mean, it's a total hazard living with me and—"

Lila tugged at her sleeve. "Herbert and Gladys, we'll leave you alone now."

"OK. We're going to take our breakfast outside for a little picnic," Herbert said, holding up a brown bag. "I'll see y'all down at the corral later."

"Nice meeting you!" Gladys said, just before she

and Herbert went out the door and ran off toward the stables, holding hands.

For a moment, the five of us just stood staring at one another. Then, all at once, we burst out laughing. "Herbert and Gladys?" Jessica said. "*Gladys?*"

"They're perfect for each other!" I said, giggling.

"Yeah, when they get married, maybe they can name their kids Marvin and Bertha!" Mandy said, and I started laughing even harder.

How had we ever gotten so wrapped up about somebody named Herbert in the first place? I might as well go home and have a crush on Winston *Egbert*, if I wanted to date someone with a goofy name. We must have been crazy, I decided. That was the first and last time I was falling for any cowboy. Nobody was worth losing your friends over.

It was almost enough to make me want to give up horseback riding. And maybe even boys.

On second thought, that might be a little too drastic. For now, I'd concentrate on avoiding singing cowboys with goofy names.

And girlfriends.


"Come on, let's go upstairs and pack," Jessica said when we got back from the rodeo exhibition and the Mexican lunch on the lawn afterward.

"Yeah, this could take a good couple of hours," Mandy said. "Your dad's going to be here at five, right?"

"Yeah," I said. "But are you guys sure you want to pack now? You might want to change into another outfit for the next half hour. You know, just to make sure you get to wear at least half of what you brought."

"You'd have to change every five minutes to do that," Ellen said, teasing.

Lila grinned. "Can we help it if we like to be prepared?"

Mandy grinned. "You're prepared, all right. For a cruise, a biking trip, a week at a ski lodge—"

"Well, the weather can change at any given moment," Jessica said.

"Yeah, it changes a lot in southern California," Mandy said. "Right."

We all laughed, and Mandy started helping me up the stairs. "Thanks," I told her, smiling.

"No problem," she replied. "But remember. We valets do accept tips."

"In your dreams," I said.

"Yeah, and in *my* dreams there really is a valet to pack up all my junk," Lila said. We walked into their room and she collapsed on the bed. "Why did I buy four Sunset Dude Ranch T-shirts? Why?" She tossed them across the room in the general direction of the closet.

"Look at it this way," Mandy said. "You have birthday presents for the next four birthday parties you get invited to."

"Three," Lila said. "I have to keep one, so I don't forget what a great weekend we had."

"Yeah," I said, as Mandy helped me walk across the room and sit on Jessica's bed. "I'm glad Mrs. Margot took those pictures of us today. It'll be fun to look back."

"There's only one problem," Jessica said, frowning. "What are we going to tell everyone when we get home? There aren't any *boys* in those pictures."

Mandy laughed. "Were there supposed to be?"

"Major boys," Lila said. "I mean, we have to have a good story to tell."

"And we have to make sure we all tell the same story," I said. "Otherwise we'll get really shown up."

"How's this?" Ellen said. "We'll tell them we had this incredible riding instructor named Herbert."

I stared at her. Mandy stared at her. Jessica's forehead creased, as if she were trying to figure out what Ellen could possibly be talking about.

"Yeah, *and*?" Lila prompted her.

Ellen shrugged. "Well, he was very handsome, and—"

"Forget it," I said, with a wave of my hand. "Nobody needs to know what happened there. We need a story with lots of boys in it."

"I know," Jessica said, snapping her fingers. "We tell everyone that—what do you know?—this group of *five boys* came to the dude ranch for the weekend. They were real cowboys from Montana. As it happened, we each met the boy of our dreams and had a fantastic time, and it was really hard to say good-bye, but we promised to write, and we're supposed to meet them back at this ranch next year!" She looked eagerly at all of us. "It's brilliant, isn't it?"

I nodded. "You are good at stories, I'll give you that."

"Yeah, and we can come up with our phony boyfriends' names on the way home, in the van," Lila said.

"I've got mine already," Mandy said. "How does this sound—Ben Steel?"

"Ooh . . ." I said. "Very cute—and tough. I'll call mine Joe . . . Grant."

"What do you guys think of this name? Johnny Lonestar. Boy, was he a hunk," Lila said with a giggle. "And then there was his identical twin, who Jessica went out with—Jimmy Lonestar."

"Hold on a second, you guys," Ellen said. "How do we explain Kimberly's sprained ankle? I mean, since she's this great rider and everything, won't it seem strange?"

"Easy," Mandy said. "We'll tell everyone she had a line-dancing accident."

I grinned at Mandy. Whether she came back into the Unicorns for good or not, I was glad she was still my friend. "It could happen to anyone," I said with a shrug. "Right, Jessica?"

She laughed. "Ankle injuries are a *lot* more common than people think."

"Maybe Herbert could carry me down to the car?" I suggested.

Jessica gave me a high five. "Now you're talking."

"You guys aren't *still* interested in him, are you?" Ellen asked. "Because Gladys seemed pretty much like his girlfriend."

"Oh, I don't know," I said. "Maybe if I changed my name to Winifred?"

As we all cracked up laughing, I felt really lucky to have such a great group of friends.

Gladys could have Herbert, as long as I had the Unicorn Club.

"It was a great weekend, but I have to admit, I'm kind of looking forward to getting home," I said to Ellen in the car. My dad had already dropped off Jessica, Lila, and Mandy, and now we were driving Ellen back to her house. "Aren't you?"

"Hmm . . ." Ellen mumbled, gazing out the window.

I giggled. "Hel-*lo*, earth to Ellen! I said, aren't you glad to be getting home? I mean, for a little peace and quiet?"

"Oh!" Ellen looked at me, startled. "What did you say? Oh, am I glad? Yeah, definitely, of course I'm glad. I mean, why wouldn't I be glad?"

I raised an eyebrow. "Ellen, are you OK? You sound a little, well, strange."

"Oh, I'm OK," she assured me. "I'm absolutely, positively OK."

"Well, all right, then," I said skeptically. "If you say so."

*What's Ellen got to hide? Find out in The Unicorn Club #9,* Ellen's Family Secret.

## SIGN UP FOR THE SWEET VALLEY HIGH® FAN CLUB!

Hey, girls! Get all the gossip on Sweet Valley High's® most popular teenagers when you join our fantastic Fan Club! As a member, you'll get all of this really cool stuff:

- Membership Card with your own personal Fan Club ID number
- A Sweet Valley High® Secret Treasure Box
- Sweet Valley High® Stationery
- Official Fan Club Pencil (for secret note writing!)
- Three Bookmarks
- A "Members Only" Door Hanger
- Two Skeins of J. & P. Coats® Embroidery Floss with flower barrette instruction leaflet
- Two editions of *The Oracle* newsletter
- Plus exclusive Sweet Valley High® product offers, special savings, contests, and much more!

---

Be the first to find out what Jessica & Elizabeth Wakefield are up to by joining the Sweet Valley High® Fan Club for the one-year membership fee of only $6.25 each for U.S. residents, $8.25 for Canadian residents (U.S. currency). Includes shipping & handling.

Send a check or money order (do not send cash) made payable to "Sweet Valley High® Fan Club" along with this form to:

**SWEET VALLEY HIGH® FAN CLUB, BOX 3919-B, SCHAUMBURG, IL 60168-3919**

NAME_____
            (Please print clearly)

ADDRESS_____

CITY_____ STATE _____ ZIP_____
                                                    (Required)

AGE_____ BIRTHDAY_____ /_____ /_____

Offer good while supplies last. Allow 6-8 weeks after check clearance for delivery. Addresses without ZIP codes cannot be honored. Offer good in USA & Canada only. Void where prohibited by law.
©1993 by Francine Pascal                                          LCI-1383-193

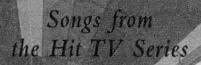

*Songs from
the Hit TV Series*

**Featuring:**

*"Rose Colored
Glasses"*

*"Lotion"*

*"Sweet Valley High
Theme"*

*Available on CD and Cassette
Wherever Music is Sold.*